# WHERE THE BLUE BEGINS

by

CHRISTOPHER MORLEY

When I saw that rage was vain,
And to sulk would nothing gain,
Turning many a trick and wile
I began to soothe and smile.

*William Blake*

LONDON
WILLIAM HEINEMANN LTD.
1928

FIRST PUBLISHED IN 1923
NEW EDITION ILLUSTRATED BY ARTHUR RACKHAM,
1925
REPRINTED, 1925
FIRST ISSUED IN THE TRAVELLERS' LIBRARY 1928

PRINTED IN GREAT BRITAIN AT THE WINDMILL PRESS,
KINGSWOOD, SURREY

# WHERE THE BLUE BEGINS

## CHAPTER ONE

G ISSING lived alone (except for his Japanese butler) in a little house in the country, in that woodland suburb region called the Canine Estates. He lived comfortably and thoughtfully, as bachelors often do. He came of a respectable family, who had always conducted themeselves calmly and without too much argument. They had bequeathed him just enough income to live on cheerfully, without display, but without having to do addition and subtraction at the end of the month and then tear up the paper lest Fuji (the butler) should see it.

It was strange, since Gissing was so pleasantly situated in life, that he got into these curious adventures that I have to relate. I do not attempt to explain it.

He had no responsibilities, not even a motor-
car, for his tastes were surprisingly simple.  If
he happened to be spending an evening at the
country club, and a rainstorm came down, he did
not worry about getting home.  He would sit by
the fire and chuckle to see the married members
creep away one by one.  He would get out his
pipe and sleep that night at the club, after tele-
phoning Fuji not to sit up for him.  When he
felt like it he used to read in bed, and even smoke
in bed.  When he went to town to the theatre,
he would spend the night at a hotel to avoid the
fatigue of the long ride on the 11.44 train.  He
chose a different hotel each time, so that it was
always an adventure.  He had a great deal of
fun.

But having fun is not quite the same as being
happy.  Even an income of 1,000 bones a year
does not answer all questions.  That charming
little house among the groves and thickets
seemed to him surrounded by strange whispers
and quiet voices.  He was uneasy.  He was rest-
less, and did not know why.  It was his theory
that discipline must be maintained in the household, so he did not tell Fuji his feelings.  Even
when he was alone, he always kept up a certain

formality in the domestic routine. Fuji would lay out his dinner jacket on the bed: he dressed, came down to the dining-room with quiet dignity, and th evening meal was served by candle-light. As long as Fuji was at work, Gissing sat carefully in the armchair by the hearth, smoking a cigar and pretending to read the paper. But as soon as the butler had gone upstairs, Gissing always kicked off his dinner suit and stiff shirt, and lay down on the hearth-rug. But he did not sleep. He would watch the wings of flame gilding the dark throat of the chimney, and his mind seemed drawn upward on that rush of light, up into the pure chill air where the moon was riding among sluggish thick floes of cloud. In the darkness he heard chiming voices, wheedling and tantalizing. One night he was walking on his little verandah. Between rafts of silver-edged clouds were channels of ocean-blue sky, conceivably deep and transparent. The air was serene, with a faint acid taste Suddenly there shrilled a soft, sweet melancholy whistle, earnestly repeated. It seemed to come from the little pond in the near-by copse. It struck him strangely. It might be anything, he thought. He ran furiously through the field, and to the brim of the pond.

He could find nothing, all was silent. Then the whistlings broke out again, all round him maddeningly. This kept on, night after night. The parson, whom he consulted, said it was only frogs; but Gissing told the constable he thought God had something to do with it.

Then willow-trees and poplars showed a pallid bronze sheen, forsythias were as yellow as scrambled eggs, maples grew knobbly with red buds. Among the fresh, bright grass came, here and there, exhilarating smells of last year's buried bones. The little upward slit at the back of Gissing's nostrils felt prickly. He thought that if he could bury it deep enough in cold beef broth it would be comforting. Several times he went out to the pantry intending to try the experiment, but every time Fuji happened to be around. Fuji was a Japanese pug, and rather correct, so Gissing was ashamed to do what he wanted to. He pretended he had come out to see that the ice-box pan had been emptied properly.

" I must get the plumber to put in a pukka drain-pipe to take the place of the pan," Gissing said to Fuji; but he knew that he had no intention of doing so. The ice-box pan was his private test of a good servant. A cook who forgot to empty it was too careless, he thought, to be a real success.

But certainly there was some curious elixir in the air. He went for walks, and as soon as he was out of sight of the house he threw down his hat and stick and ran wildly, with great exultation, over the hills and fields. " I really ought to turn all this energy into some sort of constructive work," he said to himself. No one else, he mused, seemed to enjoy life as keenly and eagerly as he did. He wondered, too, about the other sex. Did they feel these violent impulses to run, to shout, to leap and caper in the sunlight? But he was a little startled, on one of his expeditions, to see in the distance the curate rushing hotly through the underbrush, his clerical vestments dishevelled, his tongue hanging out with excitement.

" I must go to church more often," said Gissing.

In the golden light and pringling air he felt excitable and high-strung. His tail curled upward until it ached. Finally he asked Mike Terrier, who lived next door, what was wrong.

" It's spring," Mike said.

" Oh, yes, of course, jolly old spring! " said Gissing, as though this was something he had known all along, and had just forgotten for the moment.  But he didn't know.  This was his first spring, for he was only ten months old.

Outwardly he was the brisk, genial figure that the suburb knew and esteemed.  He was something of a mystery among his neighbours of the Canine Estates, because he did not go daily to business in the city, as most of them did; nor did he lead a life of brilliant amusement like the Airedales, the wealthy people whose great house was near by.  Mr. Poodle, the conscientious curate, had called several times, but was not able to learn anything definite.  There was a little card-index of parishioners, which it was Mr. Poodle's duty to fill in with details of each person's business, charitable inclinations, and what he could do to amuse a Church Sociable. The card allotted to Gissing was marked, in Mr. Poodle's neat script, *Friendly, but vague as to definite participation in Xian activities.  Has not communicated.*

But in himself, Gissing was increasingly disturbed.  Even his seizures of joy, which came as he strolled in the smooth spring air and sniffed the wild, vigorous aroma of the woodland earth, were troublesome because he did not know why he was so glad. Every morning it seemed to him that life was about to exhibit some delicious crisis in which the meaning and excellence of all things would plainly appear. He sang in the bathtub. Daily it became more difficult to maintain that decorum which Fuji expected. He felt that his life was being wasted. He wondered what ought to be done about it.

# CHAPTER TWO

I T WAS after dinner, an April evening, and Gissing slipped away from the house for a stroll. He was afraid to stay in, because he knew that if he did, Fuji would ask him again to fix the dishcloth rack in the kitchen. Fuji was very short in stature, and could not reach up to the place where the rack was screwed over the sink. Like all people whose minds are very active, Gissing hated to attend to little details like this. It was a weakness in his character. Fuji had asked him six times to fix the rack, but Gissing always pretended to forget about it. To appease his methodical butler he had written on a piece of paper *Fix Dishcloth Rack* and pinned it on his dressing-table pincushion; but he paid no attention to the memorandum.

He went out into a green April dusk. Down by the pond piped those repeated treble whistlings: they still distressed him with a mysterious unriddled summons, but Mike Terrier had told him that the secret of respect-

8

ability is to ignore whatever you don't understand. Careful observation of this maxim had
somewhat dulled the cry of that shrill queer
music. It now caused only a faint pain in his
mind. Still, he walked that way because the
little meadow by the pond was agreeably soft
underfoot. Also, when he walked close beside
the water the voices were silent. That is worth
noting, he said to himself. If you go directly
at the heart of a mystery, it ceases to be a
mystery, and becomes only a question of
drainage. (Mr. Poodle had told him that if
he had the pond and swamp drained, the frog-
song would not annoy him.) But to-night,
when the keen chirruping ceased, there was still
another sound that did not cease—a faint
appealing cry. It caused a prickling on his
shoulder-blades, it made him both angry and
tender. He pushed through the bushes. In a
little hollow were three small puppies, whining
faintly. They were cold and draggled with
mud. Someone had left them there, evidently,
to perish. They were huddled close together;
their eyes, a cloudy unspeculative blue, were
only just opened.

" This is gruesome," said Gissing, pretending

to be shocked. "Dear me, innocent pledges of sin, I dare say. Well, there is only one thing to do."

He picked them up carefully and carried them home.

"Quick, Fuji!" he said. "Warm some milk, some of the Grade A, and put a little brandy in it. I'll get the spare-room bed ready."

He rushed upstairs, wrapped the puppies in a blanket, and turned on the electric heater to take the chill from the spare-room. The little pads of their paws were ice-cold, and he filled the hot water bottle and held it carefully to their twelve feet. Their pink stomachs throbbed, and at first he feared they were dying. "They *must* not die!" he said fiercely. "If they did, it would be a matter for the police, and no end of trouble."

Fuji came up with the milk, and looked very grave when he saw the muddy footprints on the clean sheet.

"Now, Fuji," said Gissing, "do you suppose they can lap, or will we have to pour it down?"

In spite of his superior manner, Fuji was a good fellow in an emergency. It was he who suggested the fountain-pen filler. They washed

the ink out of it, and used it to drip the hot
brandy-and-milk down the puppies' throats.
Their noses, which had been icy, suddenly
became very hot and dry. Gissing feared a
fever and thought their temperatures should
be taken.

"The only thermometer we have," he said,
"is the one on the porch, with the mercury split
in two. I don't suppose that would do. Have
you a clinical thermometer, Fuji?"

Fuji felt that his employer was making too
much fuss over the matter.

"No sir," he said firmly. "They are quite
all right. A good sleep will revive them. They
will be as fit as possible in the morning."

Fuji went out into the garden to brush the
mud from his neat white jacket. His face was
inscrutable. Gissing sat by the spare-room bed
until he was sure the puppies were sleeping
correctly. He closed the door so that Fuji
would not hear him humming a lullaby. Three
Blind Mice was the only nursery song he could
remember, and he sang it over and over again.

When he tiptoed downstairs, Fuji had gone
to bed. Gissing went into his study, lit a pipe,
and walked up and down, thinking. By and

bye he wrote two letters. One was to a book-
seller in the city, asking him to send (at once)
one copy of Dr. Holt's book on the Care and
Feeding of Children, and a well-illustrated
edition of Mother Goose. The other was
to Mr. Poodle, asking him to fix a date for
the christening of Mr. Gissing's three small
nephews, who had come to live with him.

" It is lucky they are all boys," said Gissing.
" I would know nothing about bringing up
girls."

" I suppose," he added after a while, " that
I shall have to raise Fuji's wages."

Then he went into the kitchen and fixed the
dishcloth rack.

Before going to bed that night he took his
usual walk around the house. The sky was
freckled with stars. It was generally his habit
to make a tour of his property toward midnight,
to be sure everything was in good order. He
always looked in the ice-box, and admired
the cleanliness of Fuji's arrangements. The
milk bottles were properly capped with their
round cardboard tops; the cheese was never put
on the same rack with the butter; the doors
of the ice-box were carefully latched. Such

observations, and the slow twinkle of the fire in the range, deep down under the curfew layer of coals, pleased him. In the cellar he peeped into the garbage can, for it was always a satisfaction to assure himself that Fuji did not waste anything that could be used. One of the laundry tub taps was dripping, with a soft, measured tinkle: he said to himself that he really must have it attended to. All these domestic matters seemed more significant than ever when he thought of youthful innocence sleeping upstairs in the spare-room bed. His had been a selfish life hitherto, he feared. These puppies were just what he needed to take him out of himself.

Busy with these thoughts, he did not notice the ironical whistling coming from the pond. He tasted the night air with cheerful satisfaction. " At any rate, to-morrow will be a fine day," he said.

The next day it rained. But Gissing was too busy to think about the weather. Every hour or so during the night he had gone into the spare room to listen attentively to the breathing of the puppies, to pull the blanket over them, and feel

B

their noses.  It seemed to him that they were perspiring a little, and he was worried lest they catch cold.  His morning sleep (it had always been his comfortable habit to lie abed a trifle late) was interrupted about seven o'clock by a lively clamour across the hall.  The puppies were awake, perfectly restored, and while they were too young to make their wants intelligible, they plainly expected some attention.  He gave them a pair of old slippers to play with, and proceeded to his own toilet.

As he was bathing them, after breakfast, he tried to enlist Fuji's enthusiasm.  " Did you ever see such fat rascals? " he said.  " I wonder if we ought to trim their tails? "  How pink their stomachs are, and how pink and delightful between their toes!  You hold these two while I dry the other.  No, not that way!  Hold them so you support their spines.  A puppy's back is very delicate: you can't be too careful.  We'll have to do things in a rough-and-ready way until Dr. Holt's book comes.  After that we can be scientific."

Fuji did not seem very keen.  Presently, in spite of the rain, he was dispatched to the village department store to choose three small cribs and

a multitude of safety pins.  " Plenty of safety
pins is the idea," said Gissing.  " With enough
safety pins handy, children are easy to manage."

As soon as the puppies were bestowed on the
porch, in the sunshine, for their morning nap, he
telephoned to the local paperhanger.

" I want you " (he said) " to come up as soon
as you can with some nice samples of nursery
wall-paper.  A lively Mother Goose pattern
would do very well."  He had already decided
to change the spare room into a nursery.  He
telephoned the carpenter to make a gate for the
top of the stairs.  He was so busy that he did
not even have time to think of his pipe, or the
morning paper.  At last, just before lunch, he
found a breathing space.  He sat down in the
study to rest his legs, and looked for the *Times*.
It was not in its usual place on his reading-table.
At that moment the puppies woke up, and he
ran out to attend them.  He would have been
distressed if he had known that Fuji had the
paper in the kitchen and was studying the
HELP WANTED columns.

A great deal of interest was aroused in the
neighbourhood by the arrival of Gissing's
nephews, as he called them.  Several of the

ladies, who had ignored him hitherto, called, in his absence, and left extra cards. This implied (he supposed, though he was not closely versed in such niceties of society) that there was a Mrs. Gissing, and he was annoyed, for he felt certain they knew he was a bachelor. But the children were a source of nothing but pride to him. They grew with astounding rapidity, ate their food without coaxing, rarely cried at night, and gave him much amusement by their naïve ways. He was too occupied to be troubled with introspection. Indeed, his well-ordered home was very different from before. The trim lawn, in spite of his zealous efforts, was constantly littered with toys. In sheer mischief the youngsters got into his wardrobe and chewed off the tails of his evening dress coat. But he felt a satisfying dignity and happiness in his new status as head of a family.

What worried him most was the fear that Fuji would complain of this sudden addition to his duties. The butler's face was rather an enigma, particularly at meal times, when Gissing sat at the dinner table surrounded by the three puppies in their high chairs, with a spindrift of milk and prune-juice spattering generously as the youngsters plied their spoons. Fuji had arranged a series of scuppers, made of oilcloth, underneath the chairs; but in spite of this the dining-room rug, after a meal, looked much as the desert place must have after the feeding of the multitude. Fuji, who was pensive, recalled the five loaves and two fishes that produced twelve baskets of fragments. The vacuum cleaner got clogged by a surfeit of crumbs.

Gissing saw that it would be a race between heart and head. If Fuji's heart should become entangled (that is, if the innocent charms of the children should engage his affections) before his reason convinced him that the situation was now too arduous, there was some hope. He tried to ease the problem also by mental suggestion. " It is really remarkable " (he said to Fuji) " that children should give one so little trouble." As he made this remark, he was speeding hotly to and fro between the bathroom and the nursery, trying to get one tucked in bed and another undressed, while the third was lashing the tub into soapy foam.

Fuji made his habitual response, " Very good, sir." But one fears that he detected some insincerity, for the next day, which was Sunday, he gave notice.  This generally happens on a Sunday, because the papers publish more Help Wanted advertisements then than on any other day.

"I'm sorry, sir," he said.  "But when I took this place there was nothing said about three children."

This was unreasonable of Fuji.  It is very rare to have everything explained beforehand. When Adam and Eve were put into the Garden of Eden, there was nothing said about the serpent.

However, Gissing did not believe in entreating a servant to stay.  He offered to give Fuji a raise, but the butler was still determined to leave.

"My senses are very delicate," he said.  "I really cannot stand the—well, the aroma exhaled by those three children when they have had a warm bath."

"What nonsense!" cried Gissing.  "The smell of wet, healthy puppies?  Nothing is more agreeable.  You are cold-blooded: I don't believe you are fond of puppies.  Think of their wobbly black noses.  Consider how pink is the little cleft between their toes and the main cushion of their feet. Their ears are like silk. Inside their upper jaws are parallel black ridges, most remarkable. I never realised before how beautifully and carefully we are made. I am surprised that you should be so indifferent to these things."

There was a moisture in Fuji's eyes, but he left at the end of the week.

# CHAPTER THREE

A SOLITARY little path ran across the fields not far from the house. It lay deep among tall grasses and the withered brittle stalks of last autumn's goldenrod, and here Gissing rambled in the green hush of twilight, after the puppies were in bed. In less responsible days he would have lain down on his back, with all four legs upward, and cheerily shrugged and rolled to and fro, as the crisp ground-stubble was very pleasing to the spine. But now he paced soberly, the smoke from his pipe eddying just above the top of the grasses. He had much to meditate.

The dogwood tree by the house was now in flower. The blossoms, with their four curved petals, seemed to spin like tiny white propellers in the bright air. When he saw them fluttering Gissing had a happy sensation of movement. The business of those tremulous petals seemed to be thrusting his whole world forward and forward, through the viewless ocean of space.

He felt as though he were on a ship—as, indeed, we are. He had never been down to the open sea, but he had imagined it. There, he thought, there must be the satisfaction of a real horizon.

Horizons had been a great disappointment to him. In earlier days he had often slipped out of the house not long after sunrise, and had marvelled at the blue that lies upon the skyline. Here, about him, were the familiar colours of the world he knew; but yonder, on the hills, were trees and spaces of another more heavenly tint. That soft blue light, if he could reach it, must be the beginning of what his mind required.

He envied Mr. Poodle, whose cottage was on that very hillslope that rose so imperceptibly into sky. One morning he ran and ran, in the lifting day, but always the blue receded. Hot and unbuttoned, he came by the curate's house, just as the latter emerged to pick up the morning paper.

"Where does the blue begin?" Gissing panted, trying hard to keep his tongue from sliding out so wetly.

The curate looked a trifle disturbed. He feared that something unpleasant had happened, and that his assistance might be required before breakfast.

" It is going to be a warm day," he said politely, and stooped for the newspaper, as a delicate hint.

" Where does———? " began Gissing, quivering; but at that moment, looking round, he saw that it had hoaxed him again. Far away, on his own hill the other side of the village, shone the evasive colour. As usual, he had been too impetuous. He had not watched it while he ran; it had circled round behind him. He resolved to be more methodical.

The curate gave him a blank to fill in, relative to baptizing the children, and was relieved to see him hasten away.

But all this was some time ago. As he walked the meadow path, Gissing suddenly realised that lately he had had little opportunity for pursuing blue horizons. Since Fuji's departure every moment, from dawn to dusk, was occupied. In three weeks he had had three different servants, but none of them would stay. The place was too lonely, they said, and with three puppies the work was too hard. The washing, particularly, was a horrid problem. Inexperienced as a

parent, Gissing was probably too proud : he
wanted the children always to look clean and
*soigné*.  The last cook had advertised herself
as a General Houseworker, afraid of nothing;
but as soon as she saw the week's wash in the
hamper (including twenty-one grimy rompers),
she telephoned to the station for a taxi.  Gissing
wondered why it was that the working classes
were not willing to do one-half as much as he,
who had been reared to indolent ease.  Even
more, he was irritated by a suspicion of the
ice-wagon driver.  He could not prove it, but
he had an idea that this uncouth fellow obtained
a commission from the Airedales and Collies,
who had large mansions in the neighbourhood,
for luring maids from the smaller homes.  Of
course Mrs. Airedale and Mrs. Collie could
afford to pay any wages at all.  So now the best
he could do was to have Mrs. Spaniel, the char-
woman, come up from the village to do the
washing and ironing, two days a week.  The
rest of the work he undertook himself.  On
a clear afternoon, when the neighbours were
not looking, he would take his own shirts and
things down to the pond—putting them neatly
in the bottom of the red express-wagon, with

the puppies sitting on the linen, so no one would see.   While the puppies played about and hunted for tadpoles, he would wash his shirts himself.

His legs ached as he took his evening stroll—keeping within earshot of the house, so as to hear any possible outcry from the nursery.  He had been on his feet all day.  But he reflected that there was a real satisfaction in his family tasks, however gruelling.  Now, at last (he said to himself), I am really a citizen, not a mere dilettante.  Of course it is arduous.  No one who is not a parent realises, for example the extraordinary amount of buttoning and unbuttoning necessary in rearing children.  I calculate that 50,000 buttonings are required for each one before it reaches the age of even rudimentary independence.  With the energy so expended one might write a great novel or chisel a statue.  Never mind: these urchins must be my Works of Art.  If one were writing a novel, he could not delegate to a hired servant the composition of laborious chapters.

So he took his responsibility gravely.  This was partly due to the christening service, perhaps, which had gone off very charmingly.

It had not been without its embarrassments. None of the neighbouring ladies would stand as godmother, for they were secretly dubious as to the children's origin; so he had asked good Mrs. Spaniel to act in that capacity. She, a simple kindly creature, was much flattered, though certainly she can have understood very little of the symbolical rite. Gissing, filling out the form that Mr. Poodle had given him, had put down the names of an entirely imaginary brother and sister-in-law of his, "deceased," whom he asserted as the parents. He had been so busy with preparations that he did not find time, before the ceremony, to study the text of the service; and when he and Mrs. Spaniel stood beneath the font with an armful of ribboned infancy, he was frankly startled by the magnitude of the promises exacted from him. He found that, on behalf of the children, he must " renounce the devil and all his work, the vain pomp and glory of the world;" that he must pledge himself to see that these infants would " crucify the old man and utterly abolish the whole body of sin." It was rather doubtful whether they would do so, he reflected, as he felt them squirming in his arms while Mrs.

Spaniel was busy trying to keep their socks on.
When the curate exhorted him " to follow the
innocency " of these little ones, it was disconcerting to have one of them burst into a piercing
yammer, and wriggle so forcibly that it slipped
quite out of its little embroidered shift and
flannel band.  But the actual access to the holy
basin was more seemly, perhaps due to the
children imagining they were going to find
tadpoles there.  When Mr. Poodle held them
up they smiled with a vague almost bashful
simplicity; and Mrs. Spaniel could not help
murmuring " the darlings! "  The curate, less
experienced with children, had insisted on
holding all three at once, and Gissing feared lest
one of them might swarm over the surpliced
shoulder and fall splash into the font.  But
though they panted a little with excitement,
they did nothing to mar the solemn instant.
While Mrs. Spaniel was picking up the small
socks with which the floor was strewn, Gissing
was deeply moved by the poetry of the
ceremony.  He felt that something had really
been accomplished toward " burying the Old
Adam."   And if Mrs. Spaniel ever grew
disheartened at the wash-tubs, he was careful

to remind her of the beautiful phrase about the mystical washing away of sin.

They had been christened Groups, Bunks, and Yelpers, three traditional names in his family.

Indeed, he was reflecting as he walked in the dusk, Mrs. Spaniel was now his sheet anchor. Fortunately she showed signs of becoming extraordinarily attached to the puppies. On the two days a week when she came up from the village, it was even possible for him to get a little relaxation—to run down to the station for tobacco, or to lie in the hammock briefly with a book. Looking off from his airy porch, he could see the same blue distances that had always tempted him, but he felt too passive to wonder about them. He had given up the idea of trying to get any other servants. If it had been possible, he would have engaged Mrs. Spaniel to sleep in the house and be there permanently; but she had children of her own down in the shantytown quarter of the village, and had to go back to them at night. But certainly he made every effort to keep her contented. It was a long steep climb from the hollow, so he allowed her to come in a taxi and charge it to his account. Then, on condition that she would come on

Saturdays, also, to help him clean up for Sunday, he allowed her, on that day, to bring her own children, too, and all the puppies played riotously together around the place.  But this he presently discontinued, for the clamour became so deafening that the neighbours complained.  Besides, the young Spaniels, who were a little older, got Groups, Bunks, and Yelpers into noisy and careless habits of speech.

He was anxious that they should grow up refined, and was distressed by little Shaggy Spaniel having brought up the Comic Section of a Sunday paper.  With childhood's instinctive taste for primitive effects, the puppies fell in love with the coloured cartoons, and badgered him continually for " funny papers."

There is a great deal more to think about in raising children (he said to himself) than is intimated in Dr. Holt's book on *Care and Feeding*.  Even in matters that he had always taken for granted, such as fairy tales, he found perplexity.  After supper—(he now joined the children in their evening bread and milk, for after cooking them a hearty lunch of meat and gravy and potatoes and peas and the endless spinach and carrots that the doctors advise, to say nothing of the prunes, he had no energy to prepare a special dinner for himself)—after supper it was his habit to read to them, hoping to give their imaginations a little exercise before they went to bed. He was startled to find that Grimm and Hans Andersen, which he had considered as authentic classics for childhood, were full of very strong stuff — morbid sentiment, bloodshed, horror, and all manner of painful circumstance. Reading the tales aloud, he edited as he went along; but he was subject to that curious weakness that afflicts some people: reading aloud made him helplessly sleepy: after a page or so he would fall into a doze, from which he would be awakened by the crash of a lamp or some other furniture. The children, seized with that furious hilarity that usually begins just about bedtime, would race madly about the house until some breakage or a burst of tears woke him from his trance. He would thrash the mall and put them to bed howling. When they were asleep he would be touched with tender compassion, and steal in to tuck them up, admiring the innocence of each unconscious muzzle on its pillow. Sometimes, in a crisis of his problems, he thought of writing

c

to Dr. Holt for advice; but the will-power was lacking.

It is really astonishing how children can exhaust one, he used to think. Sometimes, after a long day, he was even too weary to correct their grammar. " You lay down! " Groups would admonish Yelpers, who was capering in his crib while Bunks was being lashed in with the largest size of safety pins. And Gissing, doggedly passing from one to another, was really too fatigued to reprove the verb, picked up from Mrs. Spaniel.

Fairy tales proving a disappointment, he had great hopes of encouraging them in drawing. He bought innumerable coloured crayons and stacks of scribbling paper. After supper they would all sit down around the dining-room table and he drew pictures for them. Tongues depending with concentrated excitement, the children would try to copy these pictures and colour them. In spite of having three complete sets of crayons, a full roster of colours could rarely be found at drawing time. Bunks had the violet when Groups wanted it, and so on. But still, this was often the happiest hour of the day. Gissing drew amazing trains, elephants, ships, and rainbows, with the spectrum of colours correctly arranged and blended. The children specially loved his landscapes, which were opulently tinted and magnificent in long perspectives. He found himself always colouring the far horizons a pale and haunting blue.

He was meditating these things when a shrill yammer recalled him to the house.

# CHAPTER FOUR

I N this warm summer weather Gissing slept on a little outdoor balcony that opened off the nursery. The world, rolling in her majestic seaway, heeled her gunwale slowly into the trough of space. Disked upon this bulwark, the sun rose, and promptly Gissing woke. The poplars flittered in a cool stir. Beyond the tadpole pond, through a notch in the landscape, he could see the far darkness of the hills. That fringe of woods was a railing that kept the sky from flooding over the earth.

The level sun, warily peering over the edge like a cautious marksman, fired golden volleys unerringly at him. At Once Gissing was aware and watchful. Brief truce was over: the hopeless war which Time began anew.

This was his placid hour. Light, so early, lies timidly along the ground. It steals gently from ridge to ridge; it is soft, unsure. That blue dimness, receding from bole to bole, is the skirt of Night's garment, trailing off toward

some other star.   As easily as it slips from tree
to tree, it glides from earth to Orion.

Light, which later will riot and revel and
strike pitilessly down, still is tender and tentative.   It sweeps in rosy scythe-strokes, parallel
to earth.   It gilds, where later it will burn.

Gissing lay, without stirring.   The springs of
the old couch were creaky, and the slightest
sound might arouse the children within.   Now
until they woke, was his peace.   Purposely he
had had the sleeping porch built on the eastern
side of the house.   Making the sun his alarm
clock, he prolonged the slug-a-bed luxury.   He
had procured the darkest and most opaque of
all shades for the nursery windows to cage as
long as possible in that room  Night, the silencer.
At this time of the year, the song of the mosquito
was his dreaded nightingale.   In spite of fine-
mesh screens, always one or two would get in.
Mrs. Spaniel, he feared, left the kitchen door
ajar during the day, and these Borgias of the
insect world, patiently invasive, seized their
chance.   It was a rare night when a sudden
scream did not come from the nursery every
hour or so.   " Daddy, a keeto, a keeto! " was
the anguish from one of the trio.   The other

two were up instantly, erect and yelping in their cribs, small black paws on the rail, pink stomachs candidly exposed to the winged stilleto. Lights on, and the room must be explored for the lurking foe. Scratching themselves vigourously, the fun of the chase assuaged the smart of those red welts. Gissing, wise by now, knew that after a foray the mosquito always retires to the ceiling, so he kept a step-ladder in the room. Mounted on this, he would pursue the enemy with a towel, while the children screamed with merriment. Then stomachs must be annointed with more citronella; sheets and blankets reassembled, and quiet gradually restored. Life, as parents know, can be supported on very little sleep.

But how delicious to lie there, in the morning freshness, to hear the earth stir with reviving gusto, the merriment of birds, the exuberant clink of milk-bottles set down by the back-door, the whole complex machinery of life begin anew! Gissing was amazed now, looking back upon his previous existence, to see himself so busy, so active. Few people are really lazy, he thought: what we call laziness is merely malad-justment. For in any department of life where one is genuinely interested, he will be zealous beyond belief. Certainly he had not dreamed, until he became (in a manner of speaking) a parent, that he had in him such capacity for detail.

This business of raising a family, though— had he any true aptitude for it? or was he forcing himself to go through with it? Wasn't he, moreover, incurring all the labours of parenthood without any of its proper dignity and social esteem? Mrs. Chow down the street, for instance, why did she look so sniffingly upon him when she heard the children, in the harmless uproar of their play, cry him aloud as *Daddy?* Uncle, he had intended they should call him; but that is, for beginning speech, a hard saying, embracing both a palatal and a liquid. Whereas *Da-da*—the syllables come almost unconsciously to the infant mouth. So he had encouraged it, and even felt an irrational pride in the honourable but unearned title.

A little word, *Daddy*, but one of the most potent, he was thinking. More than a word, perhaps: a great social engine: an anchor which, cast carelessly overboard, sinks deep and fast into the very bottom. The vessel rides on her hawser, and where are your blue horizons then?

But come now, isn't one horizon as good as another? And do they really remain blue when you reach them?

Unconsciously he stirred, stretching his legs deeply into the comfortable nest of his couch. The springs twanged.  Simultaneous clamours ! The puppies were awake.

They yelled to be let out from the cribs.  This was the time of the morning frolic.  Gissing had learned that there is only one way to deal with the almost inexhaustible energy of childhood.  That is, not to attempt to check it, but to encourage and draw it out.  To start the day with a rush, stimulating every possible outlet of zeal; meanwhile taking things as calmly and quietly as possible himself, sitting often to take the weight off his legs, and allowing the youngsters to wear themselves down.  This, after all, is Nature's own way with man; it is the wise parent's tactic with children.  Thus, by dusk, the puppies will have run themselves almost into a stupor; and you, if you have shrewdly husbanded your strength, may have still a little power in reserve for reading and smoking.

The before-breakfast game was conducted on regular routine. Children show their member-ship in the species by their love of strict habit.

Gissing let them yell for a few moments—as long as he thought the neighbours would endure it—while he gradually gathered strength and resolution, shook off the cowardice of bed. Then he strode into the nursery. As soon as they heard him raising the shades there was complete silence. They hastened to pull the blankets over themselves, and lay tense, faces on paws, with bright expectant upward eyes. They trembled a little with impatience. It was all he could do to restrain himself from patting the sleek heads, which always seemed to shine with extra polish after a night's rolling to and fro on the flattened pillows. But sternness was a part of the game at this moment. He solemnly unlatched and lowered the tall sides of the cribs.

He stood in the middle of the room, with a gesture of command. " Quiet now," he said. " Quiet, until I tell you! "

Yelpers could not help a small whine of intense emotion, which slipped out unintended.

The eyes of Groups and Bunks swivelled angrily toward their unlucky brother. It was his failing: in crises he always emitted haphazard sounds. But this time Gissing, with lenient forgiveness, pretended not to have heard.

He returned to the balcony, and re-entered his couch, where he lay feigning sleep. In the nursery was a terrific stillness.

It was a rule of the game that they should lie thus, in absolute quiet, until he uttered a huge imitation snore. Once, after a particularly exhausting night, he had postponed the snore too long: he fell asleep. He did not wake for an hour, and then found the tragic three also sprawling in amazing slumber. But their pillows were wet with tears. He never succumbed again, no matter how deeply tempted.

He snored. There were three sprawling thumps, a rush of feet, and a tumbling squeeze through the screen door. Then they were on the couch and upon him, with panting yelps of glee. Their hot tongues rasped busily over his face. This was the great tickling game. Remembering his theory of conserving energy, he lay passive while they rollicked and scrambled, burrowing in the bedclothes, quivering imps of absurd pleasure. All that was necessary was to give an occasional squirm, to tweak their ribs now and then, so that they believed his heart was in the sport. Really he got quite a little rest while they were scuffling. No one knew exactly what was the imagined purpose of the lark— whether he was supposed to be trying to escape from them, or they from him. Like all the best games, it had not been carefully thought out.

"Now, children," said Gissing presently. "Time to get dressed."

It was amazing how fast they were growing. Already they were beginning to take a pride in trying to dress themselves. While Gissing was in the bathroom, enjoying his cold tub (and under the stimulus of that icy sluice forming excellent resolutions for the day) the children were sitting on the nursery floor eagerly studying the intricacies of their gear. By the time he returned they would have half their garments on wrong: waist and trousers front side to rear; right shoes on left feet; buttons hopelessly mismated to buttonholes; shoelacings oddly zigzagged. It was far more trouble to permit their ambitious bungling, which must be undone and painstakingly reassembled, than to have clad them all himself, swiftly revolving and garmenting them like dolls.  But in these early hours of the day, patience still is robust.  It was his pedagogy to encourage their innocent initiatives, so long as endurance might permit.

Best of all, he enjoyed watching them clean their teeth.  It was delicious to see them, tiptoe on their hind legs at the basin, to which their noses just reached; mouths gaping wide as they scrubbed with very small toothbrushes.  They were so elated by squeezing out the toothpaste from the tube that he had not the heart to refuse them this privilege, though it was wasteful.  For they always squeezed out more than was necessary, and after a moment's brushing their mouths became choked and clotted with the pungent foam.  Much of this they swallowed, for he had not been able to teach them to rinse and gargle.  Their only idea regarding any fluid in the mouth was to swallow it; so they coughed and strangled and barked. Gissing had a theory that this toothpaste foam must be an appetizer, for he found that the more of it they swallowed, the better they ate their breakfast.

After breakfast he hurried them out into the garden before the day became too hot.  As he put a new lot of prunes to soak in cold water, he could not help reflecting how different the kitchen and pantry looked from the time of Fuji.  The ice-box pan seemed to be continually brimming over.  Somehow—due, he feared, to a laxity on Mrs. Spaniel's part—ants had got in. He was always finding them inside the ice-box, and wondered where they came from. He was amazed to find how negligent he was growing about pots and pans: he began cooking a new mess of oatmeal in the double boiler without bothering to scrape out the too adhesive remnant of the previous porridge.  He had come to the conclusion that children are tougher and more enduring than Dr. Holt will admit; and that a little carelessness in matters of hygiene and sterilization does not necessarily mean instant death.

Truly his once dainty menage was deteriorating.  He had put away his fine china, put away the linen napery, and laid the table with oil-cloth.  He had even improved upon Fuji's

invention of scuppers by a little trough, which
ran all round the brim of the table, to catch any
possible spillage.  He was horrified to observe
how inevitably callers came at the worst possible
moment.  Mr. and Mrs. Chow, for instance,
drew up one afternoon in their spick-and-span
coupe, with their intolerably spotless only child
sitting self-consciously beside them.  Groups,
Bunks, and Yelpers were just then filling the
garden with horrid clamour.  They had been
quarrelling, and one had pushed the other
two down the back steps.  Gissing, who had
attempted to find a quiet moment to scald the
ants out of the ice-box, had just rushed forth
and boxed them all.  As he stood there, angry
and waving a steaming dishclout, the Chows
appeared.  The puppies at once set upon little
Sandy Chow, and had thoroughly mauled his
starched sailor suit in the driveway before two
minutes were past.  Gissing could not help
laughing, for he suspected that there had been
a touch of malice in the Chows coming just
at that time.

He had given up his flower garden, too.  It
was all he could do to shove the lawn-mower
around, in the dusk, after the puppies were in

bed. Formerly he had found the purr of the twirling blades a soothing stimulus to thought; but nowadays he could not even think consecutively. Perhaps, he thought, the residence of the mind is in the legs, not in the head; for when your legs are thoroughly weary you can't seem to think.

So he had decided that he simply must have more help in the cooking and housework. He had instructed Mrs. Spaniel to send the washing to the steam-laundry, and spend her three days in the kitchen instead. A huge bundle had come back from the laundry, and he had paid the driver $15.98. With dismay he sorted the clean, neatly-folded garments. Here was the worthy Mrs. Spaniel's list, painstakingly written out in her straggling script:—

## MR. GISHING FAMILY WOSH

  8 towels
  6 pymjarm Mr. Gishing
12 rompers
  3 blowses
  6 cribb sheats
  1 Mr. Gishing sheat
  4 wastes

       3 wosh clothes
       2 onion sutes Mr. Gishing
       6 smal onion sutes
       4 pillo sutes
       3 sherts
      18 hankerchifs smal
       6 hankerchifs large
       8 colers
       3 overhauls
      10 bibbs
       2 table clothes (coco stane)
       1 table clothe (prun juce and eg)

After contemplating this list, Gissing went to
his desk and began to study his accounts. A
resolve was forming in his mind.

# CHAPTER FIVE

THE summer evenings sounded a very different music from that thin wheedling of April. It was now a soft steady vibration, the incessant drone and throb of locust and cricket, and sometimes the sudden rasp, dry and hard, of katydids. Gissing, in spite of his weariness, was all fidgets. He would walk round and round the house in the dark, unable to settle down to anything; tired, but incapable of rest. What is this uneasiness in the mind, he asked himself? The great sonorous drumming of the summer night was like the bruit of Time passing steadily by. Even in the soft eddy of the leaves, lifted on a drowsy creeping air, was a sound of discontent, of troublesome questioning. Through the trees he could see the lighted oblongs of neighbours' windows, or hear stridulent jazz records. Why were all others so cheerfully absorbed in the minutiæ of their lives, and he so painfully ill at ease? Sometimes, under the warm, clear

D

darkness, the noises of field and earth swelled to a kind of soft thunder: his quickened ears heard a thousand small outcries contributing to the awful energy of the world—faint chimings and whistlings in the grass, and endless flutter, rustle, and whirr.  His own body, on which hair and nails grew daily like vegetation, startled and appalled him.  Consciousness of self, that miserable ecstasy, was heavy upon him.

He envied the children, who lay upstairs sprawled under their mosquito nettings.  Immersed in living, how happily unaware of being alive!  He saw, with tenderness, how naively they looked to him as the answer and solution of their mimic problems.  But where could he find someone to be to him what he was to them?  The truth apparently was that in his inward mind he was desperately lonely.  Reading the poets by fits and starts, he suddenly realised that in their divine pages moved something of this loneliness, this exquisite unhappiness.  But these great hearts had had the consolation of setting down their moods in beautiful words, words that lived and spoke.  His own strange fever burned inexpressibly inside him.  Was he the only one who felt the challenge offered by the maddening fertility and poison of the hot sun-dazzled earth? Life, he realised, was too amazing to be frittered out in this aimless sickness of heart. There were truths and wonders to be grasped, if he could only throw off this wistful vague desire. He felt like a clumsy strummer seated at a dark shining grand piano, which he knows is capable of every glory of rolling music, yet he can only elicit a few haphazard chords.

He had his moments of arrogance, too. Ah, he was very young! This miracle of blue unblemished sky that had baffled all others since life began—he, he would unriddle it! He was inclined to sneer at his friends who took these things for granted, and did not perceive the infamous insolubility of the whole scheme. Remembering the promises made at the christening, he took the children to church; but alas, carefully analyzing his mind, he admitted that his attention had been chiefly occupied with keeping them orderly, and he had gone through the service almost automatically. Only in singing hymns did he experience a tingle of exalted feeling. But Mr. Poodle was proud of his well-trained choir, and Gissing had a feeling that the congregation was not supposed to do more than murmur the verses, for fear of spoiling the effect. In his favourite hymns he had a tendency to forget himself and let go: his vigorous tenor rang lustily. Then he realised that the backs of people's heads looked surprised. The children could not be kept quiet unless they stood up on the pews. Mr. Poodle preached rather a long sermon, and Yelpers, toward twelve-thirty, remarked in a clear tone of interested inquiry, " What time does God have dinner? "

Gissing had a painful feeling that he and Mr. Poodle did not thoroughly understand each other. The curate, who was kindness itself, called one evening, and they had a friendly chat. Gissing was pleased to find that Mr. Poodle enjoyed a cigar, and after some hesitation ventured to suggest that he still had something in the cellar. Mr. Poodle said that he didn't care for anything, but his host could not help hearing the curate's tail quite unconsciously thumping on the chair cushions. So he excused himself and brought up one of his few remaining bottles of White Horse. Mr. Poodle crossed his legs and they chatted about golf, politics, the income tax, and some of the recent books; but when Gissing turned the talk on religion, Mr. Poodle became diffident. Gissing, warmed and cheered by the vital Scotch, was perhaps too direct.

"What ought I to do to 'crucify the old man'?" he said.

Mr. Poodle was rather embarrassed.

"You must mortify the desires of the flesh," he replied. "You must dig up the old bone of sin that is buried in all our hearts."

There were many more questions Gissing wanted to ask about this, but Mr. Poodle said he really must be going, as he had a call to pay on Mr. and Mrs. Chow.

Gissing walked down the path with him, and the curate did indeed set off toward the Chows'. But Gissing wondered, for a little later he heard a cheerful canticle upraised in the open fields.

He himself was far from gay. He longed to tear out this malady from his breast. Poor dreamer, he did not know that to do so is to tear out God Himself.

"Mrs. Spaniel," he said when the laundress next came up from the village, "you are a widow, aren't you?"

" Yes, sir," she said.   " Poor Spaniel was killed by a truck, two years ago April." Her face was puzzled, but beneath her apron Gissing could see her tail wagging.

" Don't misunderstand me," he said quickly. " I've got to go away on business.   I want you to bring your children and move into this house while I'm gone.   I'll make arrangements at the bank about paying all the bills.   You can give up your outside washing and devote yourself entirely to looking after this place."

Mrs. Spaniel was so much surprised that she could not speak.   In her amazement a bright bubble dripped from the end of her curly tongue.   Hastily she caught it in her apron, and apologised.

" How long will you be away, sir? " she asked.

" I don't know.   It may be quite a long time."

" But all your beautiful things, furniture and everything," said Mrs. Spaniel.   " I'm afraid my children are a bit rough.   They're not used to living in a house like this——"

" Well," said Gissing, " you must do the best you can.   There are some things more important than furniture.   It will be good for your

children to get accustomed to refined surround-
ings, and it'll be good for my nephews to have
someone to play with. Besides, I don't want
them to grow up spoiled mollycoddles. I think
I've been fussing over them too much. If they
have good stuff in them, a little roughening
won't do any permanent harm."

"Dear me," cried Mrs. Spaniel, "what will
the neighbours think?"

"They won't," said Gissing. "I don't
doubt they'll talk, but they won't think.
Thinking is very rare. I've got to do some
myself, that's one reason why I'm going. You
know, Mrs. Spaniel, God is a horizon, not
someone sitting on a throne."

Mrs. Spaniel didn't understand this—in fact
she didn't seem to hear it. Her mind was
full of the idea that she would simply have to
have a new dress, preferably black silk, for
Sundays. Gissing, very sagacious, had already
foreseen this point.

"Let's not have any argument," he continued.
"I have planned everything. Here is some
money for immediate needs. I'll speak to them
at the bank, and they will give you a weekly
allowance. I leave you here as caretaker. Later

on I'll send you an address and you can write me how things are going."

Poor Mrs. Spaniel was bewildered. She came of very decent people, but since Spaniel took to drink, and then left her with a family to support, she had sunk in the world. She was wondering now how she could face it out with Mrs. Chow and Mrs. Fox-Terrier and the other neighbours.

" Oh, dear," she cried, " I don't know what to say, sir. Why, my boys are so disreputable-looking they haven't even a collar between them."

" Get them collars and anything else they need," said Gissing kindly. " Don't worry Mrs. Spaniel, it will be a fine thing for you. There will be a little gossip, I dare say, but we'll have to chance that. Now you had better go down to the village and make your arrangements. I'm leaving to-night."

Late that evening, after seeing Mrs. Spaniel and her brood safely installed, Gissing walked to the station with his suitcase. He felt a pang as he lifted the mosquito nettings and kissed the cool moist noses of the sleeping trio. But he comforted himself by thinking that this was no merely vulgar desertion. If he was to raise the family, he must earn some money. His modest income would not suffice for this sudden increase in expenses. Besides, he had never known what freedom meant until it was curtailed. For the past three months he had lived in ceaseless attendance; had even slept with one ear open for the children's cries. Now he owed to himself to make one great strike for peace. Wealth, he could see, was the answer. With money, everything was attainable: books, leisure for study, travel, prestige—in short, command over the physical details of life. He would go in for Big Business. Already he thrilled with a sense of power and prosperity.

The little house stood silent in the darkness as he went down the path. The night was netted with the weaving sparkle of fireflies. He stood for a moment, looking. Suddenly there came a frightened cry from the nursery.

" Daddy, a keeto, a keeto! "

He nearly turned to run back, but checked himself. No, Mrs. Spaniel was now in charge. It was up to her. Besides, he had only just enough time to catch the last train to the city.

But he sat on the cinder-speckled plush of the smoker in a mood that was hardly revelry. " By

Jove," he said to himself, " I got away just in time. Another month and I couldn't have done it."

It was midnight when he saw the lights of town, panelled in gold against a peacock sky. Acres and acres of blue darkness lay close-pressing upon the gaudy grids of light. Here one might really look at this great miracle of shadow and see its texture. The dulcet air drifted lazily in deep, silent crosstown streets. " Ah," he said, " here is where the blue begins."

# CHAPTER SIX

*" For students of the troubled heart,*
*Cities are perfect works of art."*

THERE is a city so tall that even the sky above her seems to have lifted in a cautious remove, inconceivably far. There is a city so proud, so mad, so beautiful and young, that even heaven has retreated, lest her placid purity be too nearly tempted by that brave tragic spell. In the city which is maddest of all, Gissing had come to search for sanity. In the city so strangely beautiful that she has made even poets silent, he had come to find a voice. In the city of glorious ostent and vanity, he had come to look for humility and peace.

All cities are mad: but the madness is gallant. All cities are beautiful: but the beauty is grim. Who shall tell me the truth about this one? Tragic? Even so, because wherever ambitions, vanities, and follies are multiplied by million-fold contact, calamity is there. Noble and beautiful? Aye, for even folly may have the majesty of magnitude. Hasty, cruel, shallow? Agreed, but where in this terrene orb will you find it otherwise? I know all that can be said against her; and yet in her great library of streets, vast and various as Shakespeare, is beauty enough for a lifetime. O poets, why have you been so faint ? Because she seems cynical and crass, she cries with trumpet-call to the mind of the dreamer; because she is riant and mad, she speaks to the grave sanity of the poet.

So, in a mood perhaps too consciously lofty, Gissing was meditating. It was rather impudent of him to accuse the city of being mad, for he himself, in his glee over freedom regained, was not conspicuously sane. He scoured the town in high spirits, peering into shop-windows, riding on top of 'buses, going to the Zoo, taking the rickety old steamer to the Statue of Liberty, drinking afternoon tea at the Ritz, and all that sort of thing. The first three nights in town he slept in one of the little traffic-towers that perch on stilts above Fifth Avenue. As a matter of fact, it was that one near St. Patrick's Cathedral. He had ridden up the Avenue in a taxi, intending to go to the Plaza (just for a

bit of splurge after his domestic confinement).
As the cab went by, he saw the traffic-tower,
dark and empty, and thought what a pleasant
place to sleep. So he asked the driver to let
him out at the Cathedral, and after being sure
that he was not observed, walked back to the
little turret, climbed up the ladder, and made
himself at home. He liked it so well that he
returned there the two following nights; but
he didn't sleep much, for he could not resist the
fun of startling night-hawk taxis by suddenly
flashing the red, green, and yellow lights at
them, and seeing them stop in bewilderment.
But after three nights he thought it best to
leave. It would have been awkward if the
police had discovered him.

It was time to settle down and begin work.
He had an uncle who was head of an important
business far down-town; but Gissing, with the
quixotry of youth, was determined to make his
own start in the great world of commerce. He
found a room on the top floor of a quiet brown-
stone house in the West Seventies. It was not
large, and he had to go down a flight for his
bath; the gas burner over the bed whistled; the
dust was rather startling after the clean country;

but it was cheap, and his sense of adventure more than compensated. Mrs. Purp, the landlady, pleased him greatly. She was very maternal, and urged him not to bolt his meals in armchair lunches. She put an ashtray in his room.

Gissing sent Mrs. Spaniel a postcard with a picture of the Pennsylvania Station. On it he wrote *Arrived safely. Hard at work. Love to the children.* Then he went to look for a job.

His ideas about business were very vague. All he knew was that he wished to be very wealthy and influential as soon as possible. He could have had much sound advice from his uncle, who was a member of the Union Kennel and quite a prominent dog-about-town. But Gissing had the secretive pride of inexperience. Moreover, he did not quite know what to say about his estabishment in the country. That houseful of children would need some explaining.

Those were days of brilliant heat; clear, golden, dry. The society columns in the papers assured him that everyone was out of town; but the Avenue seemed plentifully crowded with beautiful, superb creatures. Far down the gentle slopes of that glimmering roadway he could see the rolling stream of limousines, dazzles of sunlight caught on their polished flanks. A faint blue haze of gasoline fumes hung low in the bright warm air. This is the street where even the most passive are pricked by the strange lure of carnal dominion. Nothing less than a job on the Avenue itself would suit his mood, he felt.

Fortune and audacity united (as they always do) to concede his desire. He was in the beautiful department store of Beagle and Company, one of the most splendid of its kind, looking at some sand-coloured spats. In an aisle near by he heard a commotion—nothing vulgar, but still an evident stir, with repressed yelps and a genteel, horrified bustle. He hurried to the spot, and through the crowd saw someone lying on the floor. An extremely beautiful sales damsel, charmingly clad in black crêpe de chine, was supporting the victim's head, vainly fanning him. Wealthy dowagers were whining in distress. Then an ambulance clanged up to a side door, and a stretcher was brought in.

" What is it? " said Gissing to a female at the silk-stocking counter.

" One of the floorwalkers—died of heat prostration," she said, looking very much upset.

" Poor fellow," said Gissing. " You never know what will happen next, do you? " He walked away, shaking his head.

He asked the elevator attendant to direct him to the offices of the firm. On the seventh floor, down a quiet corridor behind the bedroom suites, a rosewood fence barred his way. A secretary faced him inquiringly.

" I wish to see Mr. Beagle."

" Mr. Beagle senior or Mr. Beagle junior? "

Youth cleaves to youth, said Gissing to himself.

" Mr. Beagle junior," he stated firmly.

" Have you an appointment? "

" Yes," he said.

She took his card, disappeared, and returned. " This way, please," she said.

Mr. Beagle senior must be very old indeed, he thought; for junior was distinctly grizzled. In fact (so rapidly does the mind run), Mr. Beagle senior must be near the age of retirement. Very likely (he said to himself) that will soon occur; there will be a general stepping-up among members of the firm, and that will be my chance. I wonder how much they pay a junior partner?

He almost uttered this question, as Mr. Beagle junior looked at him so inquiringly. But he caught himself in time.

" I beg your pardon for intruding," said Gissing, " but I am the new floorwalker."

" You are very kind," said Mr. Beagle junior, " but we do not need a new floorwalker."

" I beg your pardon again," said Gissing, " but you are not *au courant* with the affairs of the store. One has just died, right by the silk-stocking counter. Very bad for business."

At this moment the telephone rang, and Mr. Beagle seized it. He listened, sharply examining his caller meanwhile.

" You are right," he said, as he put down the receiver. " Well, sir, have you had any experience? "

" Not exactly of that sort," said Gissing; " but I think I understand the requirements. The tone of the store——"

" I will ask you to be here at four-thirty this afternoon," said Mr. Beagle. " We have a particular routine in regard to candidates for that position. You will readily perceive that it is a post of some importance. The floorwalker is our point of social contact with patrons——"

Gissing negligently dusted his shoes with a handkerchief.

" Pray do not apologise," he said kindly. " I am willing to congratulate with you on your good fortune. It was mere hazard that I was in the store. To-day, of course, business will be poor. But to-morrow, I think you will find——"

" At four-thirty," said Mr. Beagle, a little puzzled.

That day Gissing went without lunch. First he explored the whole building from top to bottom, until he knew the location of every department, and had the store directory firmly memorized. With almost proprietory tenderness he studied the shining goods and trinkets; noted approvingly the clerks who seemed to him specially prompt and obliging to customers; scowled a little at any sign of boredom or inattention. He heard the soft sigh of the pneumatic tubes as they received money and blew it to some distant coffer: this money, he thought, was already partly his. That square-cut creature whom he presently discerned following him was undoubtedly the store detective: he smiled to think what a pleasant anecdote this would be when he was admitted to junior partnership. Then he went, finally, to the special Masculine Shop on the fifth floor, where he bought a silk hat, a cutaway coat and waistcoat, and trousers of pearly stripe. He did not forget patent leather shoes, nor white spats. He refused the little white linen margins which the clerk wished to affix to the V of his waistcoat. That, he felt, was the ultra touch which would spoil all. The just less than perfection, how perfect it is!

It was getting late. He hurried to Penn Station, where he hired one of those little dressing booths, and put on his regalia. His tweeds, in a neat package, he checked at the parcel counter. Then he returned to the store for the important interview.

He had expected a formal talk with the two Messrs. Beagle, perhaps touching on such matters as duties, hours, salary, and so on. To his surprise he was ushered by the secretary into a charming Louis XVI saloon farther down the private corridor. There were several ladies: one was pouring tea. Mr. Beagle junior came forward. The vice-president (such was Mr. Beagle junior's rank, Gissing had learned by the sign on his door) still wore his business garb of the morning. Gissing immediately felt himself to have the advantage. But what a pleasant idea, he thought, for the members of the firm to have tea together every afternoon. He handed his hat, gloves, and stick to the secretary.

"Very kind of you to come," said Mr. Beagle. "Let me present you to my wife."

Mrs. Beagle, at the tea-urn, received him graciously.

"Cream or lemon?" she said. "Two lumps?"

This is really delightful, Gissing thought. Only on Fifth Avenue could this kind of thing happen. He looked down upon the hostess from his superior height, and smiled charmingly.

"Do you permit three?" he said. "A little weakness of mine." As a matter of fact, he hated tea so sweet; but he felt it was strategic to fix himself in Mrs. Beagle's mind as a polished eccentric.

"You must have a meringue," she said. "Ah, Mrs. Pomeranian has them. Mrs. Pomeranian, let me present Mr. Gissing."

Mrs. Pomeranian, small and plump and tightly corseted, offered the meringues, while Mrs. Beagle pressed upon him a plate with a small doily, embroidered with the arms of the store, and its motto *je maintiendrai*— referring, no doubt, to its prices. Mr. Beagle then introduced him to several more ladies in rapid succession. Gissing passed along the line, bowing slightly, but with courteous interest to each. To each one he raised his eyebrows and permitted himself a small significant smile, as though to convey that this was a moment he had long been anticipating. How different, he thought, was this life of enigmatic gaiety from the suburban drudgery of recent months. If only Mrs. Spaniel could see him now! He was about to utilise a brief pause by sipping his tea, when a white-headed patriarch suddenly appeared beside him.

" Mr. Gissing," said the vice-president, " this is my father, Mr. Beagle senior."

Gissing, by quick work, shuffled the teacup into his left paw, and the meringue plate into the crook of his elbow, so he was ready for the old gentleman's salutation. Mr. Beagle senior was indeed very old: his white hair hung over his eyes, he spoke with growling severity. Gissing's manner to the old merchant was one of respectful reassurance: he attempted to make an impression that would console: to impart—of course without saying so—the thought that though the head of the firm could not last much longer, yet he would leave his great traffic in capable care.

" Where will I find an aluminum cooking pot ? " growled the elder Beagle unexpectedly.

" In the Bargain Basement," said Gissing promptly.

" He'll do! " cried the president.

To his surprise, on looking round, Gissing saw that all the ladies had vanished. Beagle junior was grinning at him.

" You have the job, Mr. Gissing," he said. " You will pardon the harmless masquerade— we always try out a floorwalker in that way. My father thinks that if he can handle a teacup and a meringue while being introduced to ladies, he can manage anything on the main aisle downstairs. Mrs. Pomeranian, our millinery buyer, said she had never seen it better done, and she mixes with some of the swellest people in Paris."

" Nine to six, with half an hour off for lunch,"
said the senior partner, and left the room.

Gissing calmly swallowed his tea, and ate the
meringue.  He would have enjoyed another,
but the capable secretary had already removed
them.  He poured himself a second cup of tea.
Mr. Beagle junior showed signs of eagerness to
leave, but Gissing detained him.

" One moment," he said suavely.  " There is
a little matter that we have not discussed.  The
question of salary."

Mr. Beagle looked thoughtfully out of the
window.

" Thirty dollars a week," he said.

After all, Gissing thought, it will only take
four weeks to pay for what I have spent on
clothes.

# CHAPTER SEVEN

THERE was some dramatic nerve in Gissing's nature that responded eloquently to the floorwalking job. Never, in the history of Beagle and Company, had there been a floorwalker who threw so much passion and zeal into his task. The very hang of his coat-tails, even the erect carriage of his back, the rubbery way in which his feet trod the aisles, showed his sense of dignity and glamour. There seemed to be a great tradition which enriched and upheld him. Mr. Beagle senior used to stand on the little balcony at the rear of the main floor, transfixed with the pleasure of seeing Gissing move among the crowded passages. Alert, watchful, urbane, with just the ideal blend of courtesy and condescension, he raised floor-walking to a social art. Female customers asked him the way to departments they knew perfectly well, for the pleasure of hearing him direct them. Business began to improve before he had been there a week.

And how he enjoyed himself! The perfection of his bearing on the floor was no careful pose: it was due to the brimming overplus of his happiness. Happiness is surely the best teacher of good manners: only the unhappy are churlish in deportment. He was young, remember; and this was his first job. His precocious experience as a paterfamilias had added to his mien just that suggestion of unconscious gravity which is so appealing to ladies. He looked (they thought) as though he had been touched—but oh, so lightly!—by poetic sorrow or strange experience: to ask him the way to the notion counter was as much of an adventure as to meet a reigning actor at a tea. The faint cloud of melancholy that shadowed his brow may have been only due to the fact that his new boots were pinching painfully; but they did not know that.

So, quite unconsciously, he began to " establish " himself in his role, just as an actor does. At first he felt his way tentatively and with tact. Every store has its own tone and atmosphere: in a day or so he divined the characteristic *cachet* of the Beagle establishment. He saw what kind of customers were typical, and what sort of conduct they expected. And the secret of conquest being always to give people a little more than they expect, he pursued that course.   Since they expected in a floor-walker the mechanical and servile gentility of a hired puppet, he exhibited the easy, offhand simplicity of a fellow-club member.  With perfect naturalness he went out of his way to assist in their shopping concerns: gave advice in the selection of dress materials, acted as arbiter in the matching of frocks and stockings.   His taste being faultless, it often happened that the things he recommended were not the most expensive: this again endeared him to customers. When sales slips were brought to him by ladies who wished to make an exchange, he affixed his O. K. with a magnificent flourish, and with such evident pleasure, that patrons felt genuine elation, and plunged into the tumult with new enthusiasm.   It was not long before there were always people waiting for his counsel; and husbands would appear at the store to convey (a little irritably) some such message as: " Mrs. Sealyham says, please choose her a scarf that will go nicely with that brown moire dress of hers.  She says you will remember the dress." —This popularity became even a bit perplexing,

as for instance when old Mrs. Dachshund, the
store's biggest Charge Account, insisted on his
leaving his beat at a very busy time, to go up to
the tenth floor to tell her which piano he thought
had the richer tone.

Of course all this was very entertaining, and
an admirable opportunity for studying his
fellow-creatures; but it did not go very deep
into his mind. He lived for some time in a
confused glamour and glitter; surrounded by
the fascinating specious life of the store, but
drifting merely superficially upon it. The
great place, with its columns of artificial marble
and white censers of upward-shining electricity,
glimmered like a birch forest by moonlight.
Silver and jewels and silks and slippers flashed
all about him. It was a marvellous education,
for he soon learned to estimate these things at
their proper value; which is low, for they have
little to do with life itself. His work was tiring
in the extreme — merely having to remain
upright on his hind legs for such long hours was
an ordeal—but it did not penetrate to the secret
observant self of which he was always aware.
This was advantageous. If you have no intellect,
or only just enough to get along with, it does

not matter what you do.  But if you really have a mind—by which is meant that rare and curious power of reason, of imagination, and of emotion; very different from a mere fertility of conversation and intelligent curiosity—it is better not to weary and wear it out over trifles.

So, when he left the store in the evening, no matter how his legs ached, his head was clear and untarnished.  He did not hurry away at closing time.  Places where people work are particularly fascinating after the bustle is over. He loved to linger in the long aisles, to see the tumbled counters being swiftly brought to order, to hear the pungent cynicisms of the weary shop-girls.  To these, by the way, he was a bit of a mystery.  The punctilio of his manner, the extreme courtliness of his remarks, embarrassed them a little.  Behind his back they spoke of him as " The Duke " and admired him hugely; little Miss Whippet, at the stocking counter, said that he was an English noble of long pedigree, who had been unjustly deprived of his estates.

Down in the basement of this palatial store was a little dressing room and lavatory for the floorwalkers, where they doffed their formal

raiment and resumed street attire. His colleagues grumbled and hastened to depart, but
Gissing made himself entirely comfortable. In
his locker he kept a baby's bathtub, which he
leisurely filled with hot water at one of the
basins. Then he sat serenely and bathed his
feet; although it was against the rules, he often
managed to smoke a pipe while doing so. Then
he hung up his store clothes neatly, and went off
refreshed into the summer evening.

A warm rosy light floods the city at that hour.
At the foot of every crosstown street is a bonfire
of sunset. What a mood of secret smiling beset
him as he viewed the great territory of his
enjoyment! "The freedom of the city"—a
phrase he had somewhere heard—echoed in his
mind. The freedom of the city! A magnificent
saying. Electric signs, first burning wanly in the
pink air, then brightened and grew strong.
"Not light, but rather darkness visible," in that
magic hour that just holds the balance between
paling day and the spendthrift jewellery of
evening. Or, if it rained, to sit blithely on the
roof of a 'bus, revelling in the gust and whipping
of the shower. Why had no one told him of
the glory of the city? She was pride, she was

exultation, she was madness. She was what he had obscurely craved. In every line of her gallant profile he saw conquest, triumph, victory ! Empty conquest, futile triumph, loomed victory—but that was the essence of the drama. In thunderclaps of dumb ecstasy he saw her whole gigantic fabric, leaning and clamouring upward with terrible yearning. Burnt with pitiless sunlight, drenched with purple explosions of summer storm, he saw her cleansed and pure. Where were her recreant poets that they had never made these things plain?

And then after the senseless day, after its happy but meaningless triviality, the throng and mixed perfumery and silly courteous gestures, his blessed solitude! Oh solitude, that noble peace of the mind! He loved the throng and multitude of the day : he loved people : but sometimes he suspected that he loved them as God does—at a judicious distance. From his rather haphazard religious training, strange words came back to him. " For God so loved the world   .   .   ." So loved the world that—that what? That He sent someone else .   .   . Some day he must think this out. But you can't

think things out.    They think themeselves,
suddenly amazingly.    The city itself is God, he
cried.    Was not God's ultimate promise something about a city—The City of God?    Well,
but that was only symbolic language.    The city
—of course that was only a symbol for the race
—for all his kind.    The entire species, the whole
aspiration and passion and struggle, that was
God.

On the ferries, at night, after supper, was his
favourite place for meditation.    Some undeniable
instinct drew him ever and again out of the
deep and shut ravines of stone, to places where
he could feed on distance.    That is one of the
subtleties of this straight and narrow city, that
though her ways are cliffed in, they are a long
thoroughfare for the eye: there is always a far
perspective.    But best of all to go down to her
environing water, where spaces are wide: the
openness that keeps her sound and free.    Ships
had words for him: they had crossed many
horizons: fragments of that broken blue still
shone on their cutting bows.    Ferries, the most
poetical things in the city, were nearly empty
at night: he stood by the rail, saw the black
outline of the town slide by, saw the lower sky

gilded with her merriment, and was busy thinking.

Now about a God (he said to himself)—instinct tells me that there is one, for when I think about Him I find that I unconsciously wag my tail a little. But I must not reason on that basis, which is too puppyish. I like to think that there is, somewhere in this universe, an inscrutable Being of infinite wisdom, harmony, and charity, by Whom all my desires and needs would be understood; in association with Whom I would find peace, satisfaction, a lightness of heart that exceed my present understanding. Such a Being is to me quite inconceivable; yet I feel that if I met Him, I would instantly understand. I do not mean that I would understand Him: but I would understand my relationship to Him, which would be perfect. Nor do I mean that it would be always happy; merely that it would transcend anything in the way of social significance that I now experience. But I must not conclude that there is such a God, merely because it would be so pleasant if there were.

Then (he continued) is it necessary to conceive that this deity is super-canine in essence? What

I am getting at is this: in everyone I have ever known—Fuji, Mr. Poodle, Mrs. Spaniel, those maddening delightful puppies, Mrs. Purp, Mr. Beagle, even Mrs. Chow and Mrs. Sealyham and little Miss Whippet—I have always been aware that there was some mysterious point of union at which our minds could converge and entirely understand one another. No matter what our difference of breed, of training, of experience and education, provided we could meet and exchange ideas honestly there would be some satisfying point of mental fusion where we could feel our solidarity in the common mystery of life. People complain that wars are caused by and fought over trivial things. Why, of course! For it is only in trivial matters that people differ: in the deep realities they must necessarily be at one. Now I have a suspicion that in this secret sense of unity God may lurk. Is that what we mean by God, the sum total of all these instinctive understandings ? But what is the origin of this sense of kinship ? Is it not the realisation of our common subjection to laws and forces greater than ourselves ? Then, since nothing can be greater than God, He must *be* these superior mysteries. Yet He cannot be

F

greater than our minds, for our minds have imagined Him.

My mathematics is very rusty, he said to himself, but I seem to remember something about a *locus,* which was a curve or a surface every point on which satisfied some particular equation of relation among the co-ordinates. It begins to look to me as though life might be a kind of locus, whose commanding equation we call God. The points on that locus cannot conceive of the equation, yet they are subject to it. They cannot conceive of that equation, because of course it has no existence save as a law of their being. It exists only for them; they, only by it. But there it is—a perfect, potent, divine abstraction.

This carried him into a realm of disembodied thinking which his mind was not sufficiently disciplined to summarise. It is quite plain, he said to himself, that I must rub up my vanished mathematics. For certainly the mathematician comes closer to God than any other, since his mind is trained to conceive and formulate the magnificent phantoms of legality. He smiled to think that any one should presume to become a parson without having at least mastered analytical geometry.

The ferry had crossed and recrossed the river several times, but Gissing had found no conclusion for these thoughts. As the boat drew toward her slip, she passed astern of a great liner. Gissing saw the four tall tunnels loom up above the shed of the pier where she lay berthed. What was it that made his heart so stir? The perfect rake of the funnels—just that satisfying angle of slant—that, absurdly enough, was the nobility of the sight. Why, then? Let's get at the heart of this, he said. Just that little trick of the architect, useless in itself—what was it but the touch of swagger, of bravado, of defiance—going out into the vast, meaningless, unpitying sea with that dainty arrogance of build; taking the trouble to mock the senseless elements, hurricane, ice, and fog, with a 15-degree slope of masts and funnels . . . damn, what was the analogy?

It was pride, it was pride! It was the same lusty impudence that he saw in his perfect city, the city that cried out to the hearts of youth, jutted her mocking pinnacles toward sky, her clumsy turrets verticalled on gold! And God,

the God of gales and gravity, loved His children
to dare and contradict Him, to rally Him with
equations of their own.

"God, I defy you!" he cried.

## CHAPTER EIGHT

TIME is a flowing river. Happy those who allow themselves to be carried, unresisting, with the current. They float through easy days. They live, unquestioning, in the moment.

But Gissing was acutely conscious of Time. Though not subtle enough to analyse the matter acutely, he had a troublesome feeling about it. He kept checking off a series of Nows. " Now I am having my bath," he would say to himself in the morning. " Now I am dressing. Now I am on the way to the store. Now I am in the jewellery aisle, being polite to customers. Now I am having lunch." After a period in which time ran by unnoticed, he would suddenly realise a fresh *Now*, and feel uneasy at the knowledge that it would shortly dissolve into another one. He tried, vainly, to swim up-stream against the smooth impalpable fatal current. He tried to dam up Time, to deepen the stream so that he could bathe in it carelessly. Time, he said, is life; and life is God; time, then, is little bits of God. Those who waste their time in vulgarity or folly are the true atheists.

One of the things that struck him about the city was its heedlessness of Time. On every side he saw people spending it without adequate return. Perhaps he was young and doctrinaire: but he devised this theory for himself—all time is wasted that does not give you some awareness of beauty or wonder. In other words, " the days that make us happy make us wise," he said to himself, quoting Masefield's line. On that principle, he asked, how much time is wasted in this city? Well, here are some six million people. To simplify the problem (which is permitted to every philosopher) let us (he said) assume that 2,350,000 of those people have spent a day that could be called, on the whole, happy: a day in which they have had glimpses of reality; a day in which they feel satisfaction. (That was, he felt, a generous allowance.) Very well, then, that leaves 3,650,000 people whose day had been unfruitful : spent in uncongenial work, or in sorrow, suffering, and talking nonsense. This city, then, in one day, has wasted 10,000 years, or 100 centuries. One hundred centuries squandered in a day! It made him feel quite ill, and he tore up the scrap of paper on which he had been figuring.

This was a new, disconcerting way to think of the subject. We are accustomed to consider Time only as it applies to ourselves, forgetting that it is working upon everyone else simultaneously. Why, he thought with a sudden shock, if only 36,500 people in this city have had a thoroughly spendthrift and useless day, that means a net loss of a century! If the War, he said to himself, lasted over 1,500 days and involved more than 10,000,000 men, how many aeons——

He used to think about these things during quiet evenings in the top-floor room at Mrs. Purp's. Occasionally he went home at night still wearing his store clothes, because it pleased good Mrs. Purp so much. She felt that it added glamour to her house to have him do so, and always called her husband, a frightened silent creature with no collar and a humble air, up from the basement to admire. Mr. Purp's time, Gissing suspected, was irretrievably wasted—a good deal of it to judge by his dusty appearance, in rolling around in ashcans or in

the company of the neighbourhood bootlegger;
but then, he reflected, in a charitable seizure,
you must not judge other people's time-
spendings by a calculus of your own.

Perhaps he himself was growing a little
miserly in this matter. Indulging in the rare,
the sovereign luxury of thinking, he had
suddenly become aware of time's previous
fluency, and wondered why everyone else didn't
think about it as passionatey as he did. In the
privacy of his room, weary after the day afoot,
he took off his cutaway coat and trousers and
enjoyed his old habit of stretching out on the
floor for a good rest. There he would lie, not
asleep, but in a bliss of passive meditation. He
even grudged Mrs. Purp the little chats she
loved—she made a point of coming up with
clean towels when she knew he was in his room,
because she cherished hearing him talk. When
he heard her knock, he had to scramble hastily
to his feet, get on his clothes, and pretend he
had been sitting calmly in the rocking chair.
It would never do to let her find him sprawled
on the floor. She had an almost painful respect
for him. Once, when prospective lodgers were
bargaining for rooms, and he happened to be

wearing his Beagle and Company attire, she asked him to do her the favour of walking down the stairs, so that the visitors might be impressed by the gentility of the establishment.

Of course he loved to waste time—but in his own way. He gloated on the irresponsible vacancy of those evening hours, when there was nothing to be done. He lay very still, hardly even thinking, just feeling life go by. Through the open window came the lights and noises of the street. Already his domestic life seemed dim and far away. The shrill appeals of the puppies, their appalling innocent comments on existence, came but faintly to memory. Here, where life beat so much more thickly and closely, was the place to be. Though he had solved nothing, yet he seemed closer to the heart of the mystery. Entranced, he felt time flowing on toward him, endless in sweep and fulness. There is only one success, he said to himself— to be able to spend your life in your own way, and not to give others absurd maddening claims upon it. Youth, youth is the only wealth, for youth has Time in its purse!

In the store, however, philosophy was laid aside. A kind of intoxication possessed him.

Never before had old Mr. Beagle (watching delightedly from the mezzanine balcony) seen such a floorwalker. Gissing moved to and fro exulting in the great tide of shopping. He knew all the best customers by name and had learned their peculiarities. If a shower came up and Mrs. Mastiff was just leaving, he hastened to give her his arm as far as her limousine, boosting her in so expediously that not a drop of wetness fell upon her. He took care to find out the special *plat du jour* of the store's lunch room, and seized occasion to whisper to Mrs. Dachshund, whose weakness was food, that the fillet of sole was very nice to-day. Mrs. Pomeranian learned that giving Gissing a hint about some new Parisian import-ations was more effective than a half page ad. in the Sunday papers. Within a few hours, by a judicious word here and there, he would have a score of ladies hastening to the millinery salon. A pearl necklace of great value, which Mr. Beagle had rebuked the jewellery buyer for getting, because it seemed more appropriate for a dealer in precious stones than for a department store, was disposed of almost at once. Gissing casually told Mrs. Mastiff that he had heard

Mrs. Sealyham intended to buy it. As for Mrs.
Dachshund, who had had a habit of lunching
at Delmonico's, she now was to be seen taking
tiffin at Beagle's almost daily. There were many
husbands who would have been glad to shoot
him at first sight on the first of the month, had
they known who was the real cause of their woe.

Indeed, Gissing had raised floorwalking to a
new level. He was more prime minister than a
mere patroller of aisles. With sparkling eye,
with unending curiosity, tact, and attention,
he moved quietly among the throng. He
realised that shopping is the female paradise ;
that spending money she has not earned
is the only real fun an elderly and wealthy
lady can have ; and if to this primitive
shopping passion can be added the delights
of social amenity—flattery, courtesy, good-
humoured flirtation—the snare is complete.

But all this is not accomplished without
rousing the jealousy of rivals. Among the
other floorwalkers, and particularly in the
gorgeously uniformed attendant at the front
door (who was outraged by Gissing's habit of
escorting special customers to their motors)
moved anger, envy, and sneers. Gissing,

completely absorbed in the fascination of his work, was unaware of this hostility, as he was equally unaware of the amazed satisfaction of his employer. He went his way with naive and unconscious pleasure. It did not take long for his enemies to find a fulcrum for their chagrin. One evening, after closing, when he sat in the dressing room, with his feet in the usual tub of hot water, placidly reviewing the day's excitements and smoking his pipe, the superintendent burst in.

"Hey!" he exclaimed. "Don't you know smoking's forbidden? What do you want to do, get our fire insurance cancelled? Get out of here! You're fired!"

It did not occur to Gissing to question or protest. He had known perfectly well that smoking was not allowed. But he was like the stage hand behind the scenes who concluded it was all right to light a cigarette because the sign only said SMOKING FORBIDDEN, instead of SMOKING STRICTLY FORBIDDEN. He had not troubled his mind about it, one way or another.

He had drawn his salary that evening, and his first thought was, Well, at any rate I've earned enough to pay for the clothes. He had been there exactly four weeks.    Quite calmly, he lifted his feet out of the tub and began to towel them daintily.    The meticulous way he dried between his toes was infuriating to the superintendent.

" Have you any children? " Gissing asked, mildly.

" What's that to you? " snapped the other.

" I'll sell you this bathtub for a quarter.  Take it home to them.  They probably need it."

" You get out of here! " cried the angry official.

" You'd be surprised," said Gissing, " how children thrive when they're bathed regularly. Believe me I know."

He packed his formal clothes in a neat bundle, left the bathtub behind, surrendered his locker key, and walked toward the employees' door, escorted by his bristling superior.  As they passed through the empty aisles, scene of his brief triumph, he could not help gazing a little sadly.  True merchant to the last, a thought struck him.  He scribbled a note on the back of a sales slip, and left it at Miss Whippet's post by the stocking counter.  It said:—

Miss Whippet: *Show Mrs. Sealyham some of the*

*bisque sports hose, Scotch wool, size 9.  She's coming to-morrow.  Don't let her get size 8½.  They shrink.*

Mr. Gissing.

At the door he paused, relit his pipe leisurely, raised his hat to the superintendent, and strolled away.

In spite of this nonchalance, the situation was serious.  His money was at a low ebb.  All his regular income was diverted to the support of the large household in the country.  He was too proud to appeal to his wealthy uncle.  He hated also to think of Mrs. Purp's mortification if she learned that her star boarder was out of work.  By a curious irony, when he got home he found a letter from Mrs. Spaniel:—

Mr. Gissing, *dere friend, the pupeys are well, no insecks, and eat with nives and forx Groups is the fattest but Yelpers is the lowdest they send wags and lix and glad to here Daddy is doing so well in buisness with respects from*

Mrs. Spaniel.

He did not let Mrs. Purp know of the change in his condition, and every morning left his lodging at the usual time.  By some curious at-

traction he felt drawn to that down-town region
where his kinsman's office was.  This part of
the city he had not properly explored.

It was a world wholly different from Fifth
Avenue.  There was none of that sense of space
and luxury he had known on the wide slopes of
Murray Hill.  He wandered under terrific
buildings, in a breezy shadow where javelins of
colourless sunlight pierced through thin slits,
hot brilliance fell in fans and cascades over the
uneven terrace of roofs.  Here was where
husbands worked to keep Fifth Avenue going:
he wondered vaguely whether Mrs. Sealyham
had bought those stockings?  One day he saw
his uncle hurrying along Wall Street with an
intense face.  Gissing skipped into a doorway,
fearing to be recognised.  He knew that the old
fellow would insist on taking him to lunch at
the Pedigree Club, would talk endlessly, and
ask family questions.  But he was on the scent
of matters that talk could not pursue.

He perceived a sense of pressure, of
prodigious poetry and beauty and amazement.
This was a strange jungle of life.  Tall coasts
of windows stood up into the pure brilliant sky:
against their feet beat a dark surf of slums.

In one foreign street, too deeply trenched for sunlight, oranges were the only gold. The water, reaching round in two arms, came close: there was a note of husky summons in the whistles of passing craft. Almost everywhere, sharp above many smells of oils and spices, the whiff of coffee tingled his busy nose. Above one huge precipice stood a gilded statue—a boy with wings, burning in the noon. Brilliance flamed between the vanes of his pinions: the intangible thrust of that pouring light seemed about to hover him off into blue air.

The world of working husbands was more tender than that of shopping wives: even in all their business, they had left space and quietness for the dead. Sunken among the crags he found two graveyards. They were cups of placid brightness. Here, looking upward, it was like being drowned on the floor of an ocean of light. Husbands had built their offices half-way to the sky rather than disturb these. Perhaps they appreciate rest all the more, Gissing thought, because they get so little of it? Somehow he could not quite imagine a graveyard left at peace in the shopping district. It would be bad for trade, perhaps? Even the churches on the Avenue, he had noticed, were huddled up and hemmed in so tightly by the other buildings that they had scarcely room to kneel. If I ever become a parson, he said (this was a fantastic dream of his), I will insist that all churches must have a girdle of green about them, to set them apart from the world.

The two little brown churches among the cliffs had been gifted with a dignity far beyond the dream of their builders. Their pointing spires were relieved against the enormous facades of business. What other altars ever had such a reredos? Above the strepitant racket of the streets, he heard the harsh chimes of Trinity at noonday—strong jags of clangour hurled against the great sounding-boards of buildings; drifting and dying away down side alleys. There was no soft music of appeal in the bronze volleying: it was the hoarse monitory voice of rebuke. So spoke the church of old, he thought: not asking, not appealing, but imperatively, sternly, as one born to command. He thought with new respect of Mr. Sealyham, Mr. Mastiff, Mr. Dachstund, all the others who were powers

G

in these fantastic flumes of stone. They were more than mere husbands of charge accounts—they were poets. They sat at lunch on the tops of their amazing edifices, and looked off at the blue.

Day after day went by, but with a serene fatalism Gissing did nothing about hunting a job. He was willing to wait until the last dollar was broken: in the meantime he was content. You never know the soul of a city, he said, until you are down on your luck. Now, he felt, he had been here long enough to understand her. She did not give her secrets to the world of Fifth Avenue. Down here, where the deep crevice of Broadway opened out into greenness, what was the first thing he saw? Out across the harbour, turned toward open sea—Liberty! Liberty Enlightening the World, he had heard, was her full name. Some had mocked her, he had also heard. Well, what was the gist of her enlightment? Why this, surely: that Liberty could never be more than a statue: never a reality. Only a fool would expect complete liberty. He himself, with all his latitude, was not free. If he were, he would cook his meals in his room, and save money—but Mrs. Purp was strict on that point. She had spoken scathingly of two young females she ejected for just that reason. Nor was Mrs. Purp free— she was ridden by the Gas Company. So it went.

It struck him, now he was down to about three dollars, that a generous gesture toward Fortune might be valuable. When you are nearly out of money, he reasoned, to toss coins to the gods— i.e., to buy something quite unnecessary—may be propitiatory. It may start something moving in your direction. It is the touch of bravado that God relishes. In a sudden mood of tenderness, he bought two dollars' worth of toys and had them sent to the children. He smiled to think how they would frolic over the jumping rabbit. He sent Mrs. Spaniel a post-card of the Aquarium.

There is a good deal more to this business than I had realised, he said, as he walked up-town through the East Side slums that hot night. The audacity, the vitality, the magnificence, are plain enough. But I seem to see squalor, too, horror and pitiful dearth. I believe God is farther off than I thought. Look here:

if the more you know, the less you know about God, doesn't that mean that God is really enjoyed only by the completely simple—by faith, never by reason?

He gave twenty-five cents to a beggar, and said angrily: " I am not interested in a God who is known only by faith."

When he got uptown he was very tired and hungry. In spite of all Mrs. Purp's rules, he smuggled in an egg, a box of biscuits, a small packet of tea and sugar, and a tin of condensed milk. He emptied the milk into his shaving mug, and used the tin to boil water in, holding it over the gas jet. He was getting on finely when a sudden knock on the door made him jump. He spilled the hot water on his leg, and uttered a wild yell.

Mrs. Purp burst in, but she was so excited that she did not notice the egg seeping into the clean counterpane.

" Oh, Mr. Gissing," she exclaimed, " I've been waiting all the evening for you to come in. Purp and I wondered if you'd seen this in the paper to-night? Purp noticed it in the ads., but we couldn't understand what it meant."

She held out a page of classified advertising, in which he read with amazement:

## PERSONAL

If MR. GISSING, late floorwalker at Beagle and Company, will communicate with Mr. Beagle, Senior, he will hear matters greatly to his advantage.

# CHAPTER NINE

THERE had been great excitement in the private offices of Beagle and Company after Gissing's sudden disappearance. Old Mr. Beagle was furious, and hotly scolded his son. In spite of his advanced age, Beagle senior was still an autocrat and insisted on regulating the details of the great business he had built up. " You numbskull! " he shouted to Beagle junior, " that fellow was worth any dozen others in the place, and you let him be fired by a mongrel superintendent."

" But, Papa," protested the vice-president, " the superintendent had to obey the rules. You know how strict the underwriters are about smoking. Of course he should have warned Gissing, instead of discharging him——"

" Rules! " interrupted old Beagle fiercely— " Rules don't apply in a case like this. I tell you that fellow has a genius for storekeeping. Haven't I watched him on the floor? I've never

seen one like him. What's the good of your
new-fangled methods, your card indexes and
overhead charts, when you haven't even got a
record of his address? "

Growling and showing his teeth, the head
of the firm plodded stiffly downstairs and
discharged the superintendent himself. Already
he saw signs of disorganisation in the main aisle.
Miss Whippet was tearful: customers were
waiting impatiently to have exchange slips
O. K.'d: Mrs. Dachshund was turning over
some jewelled lorgnettes, but it was plain that
she was only " looking," and had no intention
to purchase.

So when, after many vain inquiries, the
advertisement reached its target, the old
gentleman welcomed Gissing with genuine
emotion.    He received him into his private
office, locked the door, and produced a decanter.
Evidently beneath his irritable moods he had
sensibilities of his own.

" I have given my life to trade," he said,
" and I have grown weary of watching the half-
hearted simpletons who imagine they can rise
to the top by thinking more about themselves
than they do about the business.    You, Mr.

Gissing, have won my heart. You see store-keeping as I do—a fine art, and absorbing passion, a beautiful, thrilling sport. It is an art as lovely and subtle as the theatre, with the same skill in wooing and charming the public."

Gissing bowed, and drank Mr. Beagle's health, to cover his astonishment. The aged merchant fixed him with a glittering eye.

" I can see that storekeeping is your genius in life. I can see that you are naturally consecrated to it. My son is a good steady fellow, but he lacks the divine gift. I am getting old. We need new fire, new brains, in the conduct of this business. I ask you to forgive the unlucky blunder we made lately, and devote yourself to us."

Gissing was very much embarrassed. He wanted to say that if he was going to consecrate himself to floorwalking, he would relish a raise in salary; but old Beagle was so tremulous and kept blowing his nose so loudly that Gissing doubted if he could make himself heard.

" I want you to take the position as General Manager," said Mr. Beagle, " with a salary of ten thousand a year."

He rose and threw open a mahogany door that

led out of his own sanctum. " Here is your office," he said.

The bewildered Gissing looked about the room—the mahogany flat-topped desk with a great sheet of plate glass shining greenly at its thick edges; an inkwell, pens and pencils, a little glass bowl full of bright paper-clips; one of those rocking blotters that are so tempting; a water cooler which just then uttered a seductive gulping bubble ; an electric fan, gently humming ; wooden trays for letters and memoranda; on one wall a great chart of names, lettered *Organisation of Personnel;* a nice domestic-looking hat-and-coat stand ; a soft green rug——

Ah, how alluring it all was!

Mr. Beagle pointed to the outer door of the room, which had a frosted pane. Through the glass the astounded floorwalker could read the words :

What a delightful little room to meditate in. From the broad windows he could see the whole

shining tideway of Fifth Avenue, passing lazily
in the warm sunlight. He turned to Mr.
Beagle, greatly moved.

The next day an advertisement appeared in
the leading papers, to this effect:—

---

### BEAGLE AND COMPANY

take pleasure in announcing to
their patrons aud friends that

#### MR. GISSING

has been admitted to the firm in
the status of *General Manager*

*Je Maintiendrai*

---

Mrs. Purp's excitement at this is easier
imagined than described. Her only fear was that
now she would lose her best lodger. She made
Purp go out and buy a new shirt and a collar;
she told Gissing, rather pathetically, that she
intended to have the whole house repapered in
the fall. The big double suite downstairs,
which could be used as a bedroom and sitting-
room, she suggested as a comfortable change.
But Gissing preferred to remain where he was.
He had grown fond of the top floor.

Certainly there was an exhilaration in his new importance and prosperity. The store buzzed with the news. At his request, Miss Whippet was promoted to the seventh floor to be his secretary. It was delightful to make his morning tour of inspection through the vast building. Mr. Hound, the store detective, loved to tell his cronies how suspiciously he had followed " The Duke " that first day. As Gissing moved through the busy departments he saw eyes following him, tails wagging. Customers were more flattered than ever by his courteous attentions. One day he even held a little luncheon party in the restaurant, at which Mrs. Dachshund, Mrs. Mastiff, and Mrs. Sealyham were his guests. He invited their husbands, but the latter were too busy to come. It would have been more prudent for them to attend. That afternoon Mrs. Dachshund, carried away by enthuisasm bought a platinum wrist-watch. Mrs. Mastiff bought a diamond dog-collar. Mrs. Sealyham, whose husband was temporarily embarrassed in Wall Street, contented herself with a Sheraton chifforobe.

But it began to be evident that his delightful little office was not going to be a shrine for quiet meditation. His vanity had been pleased by the large advertisement about him, but he suddenly realised the poison that lies in printer's ink. Almost overnight, it seemed, he had been added to ten thousand mailing lists. Little Miss Whippet, although she was fast at typewriting, was hard put to it to keep up with his correspondence. She quivered eagerly over her machine, her small paws flying. New pink ribbons gleamed through her translucent summery gorgette blouse. They were her flag of exultation at her surprising rise in life. She felt it was immensely important to get all these letters answered promptly.

And so did Gissing. In his new zeal, and in his innocent satisfaction at having entered the inner circle of Big Business, he insisted on answering everything. He did not realise that dictating letters is the quaint diversion of business men, and that most of them mean nothing. It is simply the easiest way of assuring yourself that you are busy.

This job was no sinecure. Old Mr. Beagle had so much affectionate confidence in Gissing that he referred almost everything to him for decision. Mr. Beagle junior, perhaps a little annoyed at the floorwalker's meteoric translation, spent the summer afternoons at golf. The infinite details of a great business crowded upon him. Inexperienced, he had not learned the ways in which seasoned " executives " protect themselves against useless intrusion. His telephone buzzed like a hornet. Not five minutes went by without callers or interruptions of some sort.

Most amazing of all, he found, was the miscellaneous passion for palaver displayed by Big Business. Immediately he was invited to join innumerable clubs, societies, merchants' associations. Every day would arrive letters, on heavily-embossed paper—" The Sales Managers' Club will hold a round-table discussion on Friday at one o'clock. We would greatly appreciate it if you would be with us and say a few words."—" Will you be our guest at the monthly dinner of the Fifth Avenue Guild, and give us any preachment that is on your mind? " —" The Merchandising Uplift Group of Murray Hill will meet at the Commodore for an informal lunch. It has been suggested that you contribute to the discussion on Underwriting Overhead."—" The Executives Association plans a clambake and barbecue at the Barking Rock Country Club. Around the bonfire a few impromptu remarks on Business Cycles will be called for. May we count on you? "—" Will you address the Convention of Knitted Body-garment Buyers, on whatever topic is nearest your heart? "—" Will you write for *Bunion and Callous*, the trade organ of the Floorwalkers' Union a thousand-word review of your career? " —" Will you broadcast a twenty-minute talk on Department Store Ethics, at the radio station in Newark? 250,000 radio fans will be listening in."

New to the strange and high-spirited world of " executives," it was natural that Gissing did not realise that the net importance of this kind of thing was absolute zero. It did not strike him as odd, perhaps, that merchants did not care to go on a junket or plan a congenial dinner without pretending to themselves that it had some business significance. But, having been so amazingly lifted into this atmosphere of great affairs, he felt it was his duty to the store to play the game according to the established rules. He was borne along on a roaring spate of conferences, telephone calls, appointments,

Rotarian lunches, Chamber of Commerce dinners, picnics to talk tariff, house-parties to discuss demurrage, tennis tournaments to settle the sales-tax, golf foursomes to regulate price-maintenance. Of all these matters he knew nothing whatever; and he also saw that as far as the business of Beagle and Company was concerned it would be better not to waste his time on such side-issues. The way he could really be of service was in the store itself, tactfully lubricating that complicated engine of goods and personalities. But he learned to utter, when called upon, a few suave generalities, barbed with a rollicking story. This made him always welcome. He was of a studious disposition, and liked to examine this queer territory of life with an unprejudiced eye. After all, his inward secret purpose had nothing to do with the success or failure of retail trade. He was still seeking a horizon that would stay blue when he reached it.

More and more he was interested to perceive how transparent the mummery business was. He was interested to note how persistently men fled from success, how carefully most of them avoided the obvious principles of utility, honesty, prudence, and courtesy, which are

inevitably rewarded. These sagacious humour-
ous fellows who were amusing themselves with
twaddling trade apothegms and ridiculous
banqueteering solemnities, surely they were
aware that this had no bearing upon their own
jobs? He suspected that it was all feverish
anodyne to still some inward unease. Since they
must (not being fools) be aware that these antics
were mere subtraction of time from their business, the obvious conclusion was, they were not
happy with business. There was some strange
wistfulness in the conduct of Big Business Dogs,
he thought. Under the pretence of transacting
affairs, they were really trying to discover something that had eluded them.

The same thing, strangely enough, seemed
to be going on in a sphere of which he knew
nothing—the world of art. He gathered from
the papers that writers, painters, musicians, were
holding shindies almost every night, at which
delightful rebels, too busy to occupy themselves
with actual creation, talked charmingly about
their plans. Poets were reading poems
incessantly, forgetting to write any. Much of
the newspaper comment on literature made him
shudder, for though this was a province quite

strange to him, he had sound instincts. He
discerned fatal ignorance and absurdity between
the pompous lines. Yet, in its own way, it
seemed a bold and honest ignorance. Were
these, too, like the wistful executives, seeking
where the blue begins?

But what was this strange agitation that
forbade his fellow-creatures from enjoying the
one thing that makes achievement possible—
Solitude? He himself, so happy to be left alone
—was no one else like that? And yet this
very solitude that he craved and revelled
in was, by a sublime paradox, haunted by
mysterious loneliness. He felt sometimes as
though his heart had been broken off from some
great whole, to which it yearned to be reunited.
It felt like a bone that had been buried, which
God would some day dig up. Sometimes, in
his caninomorphic conception of deity, he felt
near him the thunder of those mighty paws.
In rare moments of silence he gazed from his
office window upon the sun-gilded, tempting
city. Her madness was upon him—her splendid
craze of haste, ambition, pride. Yet he
wondered. This God he needed, this liberating

H

horizon, was it after all in the cleverest of hiding-places—in himself? Was it in his own undeluded heart?

Miss Whippet came scurrying in to say that the Display Manager begged him to attend a conference. The question of apportioning window space to the various departments was to be reconsidered. Also, the book department had protested having rental charged against them for books exhibited merely to add a finishing touch to a furniture display. Other agenda : the Personnel Director wished an appointment to discuss the ruling against sales-bitches bobbing their hair. The Commissary Department wished to present revised figures as to the economy that would be effected by putting the employees' cafeteria on the same floor as the store's restaurant. He must decide whether early closing on Saturdays would continue until Labour Day.

As he went about these and a hundred other fascinating trivialities, he had a painful sense of treachery to Mr. Beagle senior. The old gentleman was so touchingly certain that he had found in him the ideal shoulders on which to unload his honourable and crushing burden.

With more than paternal pride old Beagle saw Gissing, evidently urbane and competent, cheerfully circulating here and there. The shy angel of doubt that lay deep in Gissing's cider-coloured eye, the proprietor did not come near enough to observe.

If there is tragedy in our story, alas here it is. Gissing, incorrigible seceder from responsibilities that did not touch his soul, did not dare tell his benefactor the horrid truth. But the worm was in his heart. Late one night, in his room at Mrs. Purp's, he wrote a letter to Mr. Poodle. After mailing it at a street-box, he had a sudden pang. To the dreamer, decisions are fearful. Then he shook himself and ran lightly to a little lunchroom on Amsterdam Avenue, where he enjoyed doughnuts and iced tea. His mind was resolved. The doughnuts, by a simple symbolism, made him think of Rotary Clubs, also of millstones. No, he must be a fugitive from honour, from wealth, from Chambers of Commerce. Fugitive from all save his own instinct. Those who have bound themselves are only too eager to see the chains on others. There was no use attempting to explain to Mr.

Beagle—the dear old creature would not understand.

The next day, after happily and busily discharging his duties, and staying late to clean up his desk, Gissing left Beagle and Company for good. The only thing that worried him, as he looked round his comfortable office for the last time, was the thought of little Miss Whippet's chagrin when she found her new promotion at an end. She had taken such delight in their mutual dignity. On the filing cabinet beside her typewriter desk was a pink geranium in a pot, which she watered every morning. He could not resist pulling out a drawer of her desk, and smiled gently to see the careful neatness of its compartments, with all her odds and ends usefully arranged. The ink-eraser, with an absurd little whisk attached to it for brushing away fragments of rubbed paper; the fascicle of sharpened pencils held together by an elastic band; the tiny phial of typewriter oil; a small box of peppermints; a crumpled handkerchief; the stenographic notebook with a pencil inserted at the blank page, so as to be ready for instant service the next day; the long paper-cutter for slitting envelopes; her memorandum pad, on which was written *Remind Mr. G. of Window Display Luncheon*—it seemed cruel to deprive her of all these innocent amusements in which she delighted so much. And yet he could not go on as a General Manager simply for the happiness of Miss Whippet.

In the foliage of the geranium, where he knew she would find it the first thing in the morning, he left a note:—

MISS WHIPPET: I am leaving the store to-night and will not be back. Please notify Mr. Beagle. Explain to him that I shall never take a position with one of his competitors ; I am leaving not because I didn't enjoy the job, but because if I stayed longer I might enjoy it too much. Tell Mr. Beagle that I specially urge him to retain you as assistant to the new Manager, whoever that may be. You are entirely competent to attend to the routine, and the new Manager can spend all his time at business lunches.

Please inform the Display Managers' Club that I can't speak at their meeting to-morrow.

I wish you all possible good fortune.

MR. GISSING.

As he passed through the dim and silent aisles

of the store, he surveyed them again with mixed emotions. Here he might, apparently, have been king. But he had no very poignant regret. Another of his numerous selves, he reflected, had committed suicide. That was the right idea: to keep sloughing them off, throwing overboard the unreal and factitious Gissings, paring them down until he discovered the genuine and inalienable creature.

And so, for the second time he made a stealthy exit from the employees' door.

Four days later he read in the paper of old Mr. Beagle's death. There can be no doubt about it. The merchant died of a broken heart.

# CHAPTER TEN

M R. POODLE'S reply was disappointing. He said:—

*St. Bernard's Rectory,*
September 1st.

My dear Mr. Gissing:

I regret that I cannot conscientiously see my way to writing to the Bishop in your behalf. Any testimonial I could compose would be doubtful at best, for I cannot agree with you that the Church is your true vocation. I do not believe that one who has deserted his family, as you have, and whose record (even on the most charitable interpretation) cannot be described as other than eccentric, would be useful in Holy Orders. You say that your life in the city has been a great purgation. If so, I suggest that you return and take up the burdens laid upon you. It has meant great mortification to me that one of my own parish has been the cause of these painful rumours that have afflicted our quiet community. Notwithstanding, I wish you well, and hope that chastening experience may bring you peace.

Very truly yours,

J. Rover Poodle.

Gissing meditated this letter in the silence of a long evening in his room. He brought to the problem his favourite aid to clear thinking—strong coffee mixed with condensed milk. Mrs. Purp had made concession to his peculiarities when he had risen so high in the world: better to break any rules, she thought, than lose so notable a tenant. She had even installed a small gas-plate for him, so that he could brew his morning and evening coffee.

So he took counsel with his percolator, whose bubbling was a sound he found both soothing and stimulating. He regarded it as a kind of private oracle, with a calm voice of its own. He listened attentively as he waited for the liquid to darken. *Appeal—to—the—Bishop, Appeal—to—the—Bishop,* seemed to be the speech of the jetting gurgitation under the glass lid.

He determined to act upon this, and lay his case before Bishop Borzoi even without the introduction he had hoped for. Fortunately he still had some sheets of Beagle and Company notepaper, with the engraved lettering and *Office of the General Manager* embossed thereon. He was in some doubt as to the proper formality and style of address in communicating

with a Bishop: was it " Very Reverend," or
" Right Reverend " ? and which of these
indicated a superior grade of reverendability?
But he decided that a masculine frankness would
not be amiss. He wrote:—

VERY RIGHT REVEREND BISHOP BORZOI,
Dear Bishop:—

May one of the least of your admirers solicit an
interview with your very right reverence, to discuss
matters pertaining to religion, theology, and a
possible vacancy in the Church? If there are any sees
outstanding it would be a favour. This is very
urgent. I enclose a stamped addressed envelope.

Respectfully yours,

MR. GISSING.

A prompt reply from the Bishop's secretary
granted him an appointment.

Scrupulously attired in his tail-coat and silk
hat, Gissing proceeded toward the rendezvous.
To tell the truth, he was nervous: his mind
flitted uneasily among possible embarrassments.
Suppose Mr. Poodle had writen to the Bishop to
prejudice his application? Another, but more
absurd idea troubled him. One of the problems
in visiting the houses of the Great (he had

learned in his brief career in Big Business) is to find the door-bell. It is usually mysteriously concealed. Suppose he should have to peer hopelessly about the vestibule, in a shameful and suspicious manner, until some flunkey came out to chide? In the sunny park below the Cathedral he saw nurses sitting by their puppy-carriages; for an instant he almost envied their gross tranquillity. *They* have not got (he said to himself) to call on a Bishop!

He was early, so he strolled for a few minutes in the park that lies beneath that rocky scarp. On the summit, clear-surging against the blue, the great church rode like a ship on a long ridge of sea. The angel with a trumpet on the jut of the roof was like a valiant seaman in the crow's nest. His agitation was calmed by this noble sight. Yes, he said, the Church is a ship behind whose bulwarks I will find rest. She sails an unworldly sea: her crew are exempt from earthly ambition and fallacy.

He ran nimbly up the long steps that scale the cliff, and approached the episcopal residence. The bell was plainly visible. He rang, and presently came a tidy little housemaid. He had meditated a form of words. It would be absurd to say " Is the Bishop in? " for he knew the Bishop *was* in. So he said " This is Mr. Gissing. I think the Bishop is expecting me."

Bishop Borzoi was an impressive figure— immensely tall and slender, with long, narrow ascetic face and curly white hair. He was surprisingly cordial.

" Ah, Mr. Gissing? " he said. " Sit down, sir. I know Beagle and Company very well. Too well, in fact—Mrs. Borzoi has an account there."

Gissing, feeling rather aghast and tentative, had no comment ready. He was still worrying a little as to the proper mode of address.

" It is very pleasant to find you Influential Merchants interested in the Church," continued the Bishop. " I often thought of approaching the late Mr. Beagle on the subject of a small contribution to the cathedral. Indeed, I have spent so much in your store that it would be only a fair return. Mr. Collie, of Greyhound, Collie and Company, has been very handsome with us: he has just provided for repaving the choir."

Gissing began to fear that the object of his visit had perhaps been misunderstood, but the prelate's eyes were bright with benignant enthusiasm and he dared not interrupt.

"You inquired most kindly in your letter as to a possible vacancy in the Church. Indeed there is a niche in the transept that I should be happy to see filled. It is intended for some kind of memorial statue, and perhaps, in honour of the late Mr. Beagle——"

"I must explain, Sir Bishop," said Gissing, very much disturbed, "that I have left Beagle and Company. The contribution I wish to make to the Church is not a decorative one, I fear. It is myself."

"Yourself?" queried the Bishop, politely puzzled.

"Yes," stammered Gissing, "I—in fact, I am hoping to—to enter the ministry."

The Bishop was plainly amazed, and his long, aristocratic nose seemed longer than ever as he gazed keenly at his caller.

"But have you had any formal training in theology?"

"None, right reverend Bishop," said Gissing. "But it's this way," and, incoherently at first, but with increasing energy and copious eloquence, he poured out the story of his mental struggles.

"This is singularly interesting," said the Bishop at length. " I can see that you are wholly lacking in the rudiments of divinity. Of modern exegesis and criticism you are quite innocent. But you evidently have something which is much rarer—what the Quakers call a *concern*. Of course you should really go to the theological seminary and establish this naif intuitive mysticism upon a disciplined basis. You will realise that we churchmen can only meet modern rationalism by a rationalism of our own—by a philosophical scholarship which is unshakable. I do not suppose that you can even harmonise the Gospels? "

Gissing ruefully admitted his ignorance.

"Well, at least I must make sure of a few fundamentals," said the Bishop. " Of course a symbological latitude is permissible, but there are some essentials of dogma and creed that may not be foregone."

He subjected the candidate to a rapid catechism. Gissing, in a state of mind curiously mingled of excitement and awe, found himself assenting to much that, in a calmer moment, he would hardly have admitted ; but having plunged so deep into the affair he felt it would be the height of discourtesy to give negative answers to any of the Bishop's queries. By dint of hasty mental adjustments and symbolic interpretations, he satisfied his conscience.

"It is very irregular," the Bishop admitted, "but I must confess that your case interests me greatly. Of course I cannot admit you to ordination until you have passed through the regular theological curriculum. Yet I find you singularly apt for one without proper training."

He brooded a while, fixing the candidate with a clear darkly burning eye.

"It struck me that you were a trifle vague upon some of the Articles of Religion, and the Table of Kindred and Affinity. You must remember that these articles are not to be subjected to your own sense or comment, but must be taken in the literal and grammatical meaning. However, you show outward and visible signs of an inward grace. It so happens that I know of a small chapel, in the country, that has been closed for lack of a minister. I can put you in charge there as lay reader."

Gissing's face showed his elation.

"And wear a cassock?" he cried.

"Certainly not," said the Bishop sternly. "Not even a surplice. You must remember you have not been ordained. If you are serious in your zeal, you must work your way up gradually, beginning at the bottom."

"I have seen some of your cloth with a little purple dicky, which looks very well in the aperture of the waistcoat," said Gissing humbly. "How long would it take me to work up to that?"

Bishop Borzoi, who had a sense of humour, laughed genially.

"Look here," he said. "It's a fine afternoon: I'll order my car and we'll drive out to Dalmatian Heights. I'll show you your chapel, and tell you exactly what your duties will be."

Gissing was startled. Dalmatian Heights was only a few miles from the Canine Estates. If the news should reach Mr. Poodle . . .

"Sir Bishop," he said nervously, "I begin to fear that perhaps after all I am unworthy. Now about those Articles of Religion: I may perhaps have given some of them a conjectural and commentating assent. Possibly I have presumed too far——"

The Bishop was already looking forward to a ride into the country with his unusual novice.

" Not at all, not at all," he said cheerily. " In a mere lay reader, a slight laxity is allowable. You understand, of course, that you are expressly restricted from the pulpit. You will have to read the lessons, conduct the service, and may address the congregation upon matters not homiletic nor doctrinal; preaching and actual entry into the pulpit are defended. But I see excellent possibility in you. Perform the duties punctually in this very lowly office, and high ranks of service in the church militant will be open."

He put on a very fine shovel-hat and led the way to his large touring car.

It was a very uncomfortable ride for Gissing. A silk hat is the least stable apparel for swift motoring, and the chaffeur drove at high speed. The Bishop, leaning back in the open tonneau, crossed one delicately slender shank over another, gazed in a kind of ecstasy at the countryside, and talked gaily about his days as a young curate. Gissing sat holding his hat on. He saw only too well that, by the humiliating oddity of chance, they were going to take the road that led exactly passed his own house. He could only hope that Mrs. Spaniel and the various children would not be visible, for explanations would be too complicated. Desperately he praised the view to be obtained on another road, but Bishop Borzoi was too interested in his own topic to pay much attention.

"By the way," said the latter, as they drew near to the familiar region, "I must introduce you to Miss Airedale. She lives in the big place on the hill over there. Her family always used to attend what I will now call *your* chapel; she is a very ardent churchgoer, and it was a sincere grief to her when the place had to be closed. You will find her a great aid and comfort; not only that, she is—what one does not always find in the devouter members of her sex—young and beautiful. I think I understood you to say you are a bachelor?"

They were approaching the last turning at which it was still possible to avoid the fatal road, and Gissing's attention was divided.

"Yes, after a fashion," he replied. "Bishop, do you know that road down into the valley? The view is really superb—Yes, that road—Oh, no, I am a bachelor——"

I

It was too late. The chaffeur, unconscious of this private crisis, was spinning along the homeward way. With a tender emotion Gissing saw the spires of the poplar trees, the hemlocks down beyond the pond, the fringe of woods that concealed the house until you were quite upon it——

The car swerved suddenly and the driver only saved it by a quick and canny manœuvre from going down the bank. He came to a stop, and almost from underneath the rear wheels appeared a scuffling, dusty group of youngsters who had been playing in the road. There they were—Bunks, Groups, and Yelpers (inordinately grown!) and two of the Spaniels. Their clothes were deplorable, their faces grimed, their legs covered with burrs, their whole demeanour was ragamuffin and wild; yet Gissing felt a pang of pride to see his godchildren's keen, independent bearing contrasted with the rowdier, disreputable look of the young Spaniels. Quickly he averted his head to escape recognition. But the urchins were all gaping at the Bishop's shovel hat.

" Hot dog! " cried Yelpers. " Some hat! "

To his horror, Gissing now saw Mrs. Spaniel,

hastening in alarm down from the house, spilling potatoes from her apron as she ran. He hurriedly urged the driver to proceed.

"What terrible looking children," observed the Bishop, who seemed fascinated by their stare. "Really, my good sister," he said to Mrs. Spaniel, who was now panting by the running board; "you must keep them off the road or someone will get hurt."

Gissing was looking for an imaginary object on the floor of the car. To his great relief he heard the roar of the motor as they started again. But he sat up a little too soon. A simultaneous roar of "Daddy!" burst from the trio.

"What was that they were shouting at us?" inquired the Bishop, looking back.

Gissing shook his head. He was too overcome to speak.

# CHAPTER ELEVEN

THE little chapel at Dalmatian Heights sat upon a hill, among a grove of pines, the most romantic of all trees. Life, a powerful but clumsy dramatist, does not reject the most claptrap " situations," which a sophisticated playwright would discard as too obvious. For this sandy plateau, strewn with satiny pine-needles, was the very horizon that had looked so blue and beckoning from the little house by the pond. Not far away was the great Airedale estate, which Gissing had known only at an admiring distance—and now he was living there as an honoured guest.

The Bishop had taken him to call upon the Airedales; and they, delighted that the chapel was to be re-opened, had insisted upon his staying with them. The chapel, in fact, was a special interest with Mr. Airedale, who had been a leading contributor toward its erection. Gissing was finding that life seemed to be continually putting him into false positions; and now he discovered, somewhat to his chagrin, that the lovely little shrine of St. Spitz, whose stained windows glowed like rubies in its cloister of dark trees, was rather a fashionable hobby among the wealthy land-owners of Dalmatian Hills. It had been closed all summer, and they had missed it. The Bishop, in his airy and indefinite way, had not made it quite plain that Gissing was only a lay reader; and in spite of his embarrassed disclaimers, he found himself introduced by Mr. Airedale to the country-house clique as the new " vicar."

But at any rate it was lucky that the Airedales had insisted on taking him in as guest; for he had learned from the Bishop (just as the latter was leaving) that there was no stipend attached to the office of lay reader. Fortunately he still had much of the money he had saved from his salary as General Manager. And whatever sense of anomaly he felt was quickly assuaged by the extraordinary comfort and novelty of his environment. In the great Airedale mansion he experienced for the first time that ultimate triumph of civilization—a cup of tea served in bed before breakfast, with slices of bread-and-butter of tenuous and amazing fragile thinness.

He was pleased, too, with the deference paid him as the representative of the cloth, even though it compelled him to a solemnity he did not inwardly feel. But most of all, undoubtedly, he was captivated by the loveliness and warmth of Miss Airedale.

The Bishop had not erred. Admiring the Aristocratic Roman trend of her brow and nose; the proud, inquisitive carriage of her somewhat rectangular head; her admirable, vigorous figure and clear topaz eyes, Gissing was aware of something he had not experienced before—a disturbance both urgent and agreeable, in which the intellect seemed to play little part. He was startled by the strength of her attractiveness, amazed to learn how pleasing it was to be in her company. She was very young and brisk: wore clothes of a smart sporting cut, and was (he thought) quite divine in her riding breeches. But she was also completely devoted to the chapel, where she played the music on Sundays. She was a volatile creature, full of mischievous surprise: at their first music practice, after playing over some hymns on the pipe-organ, she burst into jazz, filling the quiet grove with the clamorous syncope of *Paddy-Paws,* a favourite song that summer.

So into the brilliant life of the Airedales and their friends he found himself suddenly pitchforked. In spite of the oddity of the situation, and of occasional anxiety when he considered the possibility of Mr. Poodle finding him out, he was very happy. This was not quite what he had expected, but he was always adaptable. Miss Airedale was an enchanting companion. In the privacy of his bedroom he measured himself for a pair of riding breeches and wrote to his tailor in town to have them made as soon as possible. He served the little chapel assiduously, though he felt it better to conceal from the Airedales the fact that he went there every day He suspected they would think him slightly mad if they knew, so he used to pretend that he had business in town. Then he would slip away to the balsam-scented hilltop and be perfectly happy sweeping the chapel floor, dusting the pews, polishing the brasswork, rearranging the hymnals in the racks. He arranged with the milkman to leave a bottle of milk and some cinnamon buns at the chapel gate every morning, so he had a cheerful and stealthy little lunch in the vestry-room, though always a trifle nervous lest some of his parishoners should discover him.

He practised reading the lessons aloud at the brass lectern, and discovered how easy is dramatic elocution when you are alone. He wished it were possible to hold a service daily. For the first time he was able to sing hymns as loud as he liked. Miss Airedale played the organ with emphatic fervour, and the congregation, after a little hesitation, enjoyed the lusty sincerity of a hymn well trolled. Some of his flock, who had previously relished taking part in the general routine of the service, were disappointed by his zeal, for Gissing insisted on doing everything himself. He rang the bell, ushered the congregation to their seats, read the service, recited the Quadrupeds' Creed, led the choir, gave out as many announcements as he could devise, took up the collection, and at the close skipped out through the vestry and was ready and beaming in the porch before the nimblest worshipper had reached the door. On his first Sunday, indeed, he carried enthusiasm rather too far: in an innocent eagerness to prolong the service as much as possible, and being too excited to realise quite what he was doing, he went through the complete list of supplications for all possible occasions. The congregation were startled to find themselves praying simultaneously both for rain and for fair weather.

In a cupboard in the vestry-room he had found an old surplice hanging; he took it down, tried it on before the mirror, and wistfully put it back. To this symbolic vestment his mind returned as he sat solitary under the pine-trees, looking down upon the valley of home. It was the season of goldenrod and aster on the hill-sides: a hot swooning silence lay upon the late afternoon. The weight and closeness of the air had struck even the insects dumb. Under the pines, generally so murmurous, there was something almost gruesome in the blank stillness: a suspension so absolute that the ears felt dull and sealed. He tried, involuntarily, to listen more clearly, to know if this uncanny hush were really so. There was a sense of being imprisoned, but only most delicately, in a spell, which some sudden cracking might disrupt.

The surplice tempted him strongly, for it

suggested the service he felt impelled to
deliver, against the Bishop's orders. For the
beautiful chapel in the tiny glade was, somehow,
false : or, at any rate, false for him. The
architect had made it a dainty poem in stone
and polished wood, but somehow God had
evaded the neat little trap. Moreover, the God
his well-bred congregation worshipped, the old
traditionally-imagined snow-white St. Bernard
with radiant jowels of tenderness, shining dew-
laps of love; paternal, omnipotent, calm—this
deity, though sublime in its way, was too
plainly an extension of their own desires.
His prominent parishoners—Mr. Dobermann-
Pinscher, Mrs. Griffon, Mrs. Retriever; even
the delightful Mr. Airedale himself—was it
not likely that they esteemed a deity everlast-
ingly forgiving because they themselves felt
need of forgiveness ? He had been deeply
shocked by the docility with which they followed
the codes of the service: even when he had
committed his blunder of the contradictory
prayers, they had murmured the words
automatically, without protest. To the terrific
solemnities of the Litany they had made the
responses with prompt gabbling precision, and

with a rapidity that frankly implied impatience to take the strain off their knees.

Somehow he felt that to account for a world of unutterable strangeness they had invented a God far too cheaply simple. His mood was certainly not one of ribald easy scoff. It was they (he assured himself) whose theology was essentially cynical; not he. He was a little weary of this just, charitable, consoling, hebdomadal God; this God who might be sufficiently honoured by a decorously memorized ritual. Yet was he too shallow? Was it not seemly that his fellows, bound on this dark, desperate venture of living, should console themselves with decent self-hypnosis?

No, he thought. No, it was not entirely seemly. It they pretended that their God was the highest thing knowable, then they must bring to His worship the highest possible powers of the mind. He had a strange yearning for a God less lazily conceived : a God perhaps inclement, awful, master of inscrutable principles. Yet was it desirable to shake his congregation's belief in their traditional divinity? He thought of them—so amiable, amusing, spirited and generous, but utterly untrained for abstract imaginative thought on any subject whatever. His own strange surmisings about deity would only shock and horrify them. And, after all, was it not exactly their simplicity that made them lovable? The great laws of truth would work their own destinies without assistance from him! Even if these pleasant creatures did not genuinely believe the rites they so politely observed (he knew they did not, for *belief* is an intellectual process of extraordinary range and depth), was it not socially useful that they should pretend to do so?

And yet—with another painful swing of the mind—was it necessary that Truth should be worshipped with the aid of such astonishingly transparent formalisms, hoaxes, and mummeries?? Alas, it seemed that this was an old, old struggle that must be troublesomely fought out again and again down the generations. Prophets were twice stoned—first in anger; then, after their death, with a handsome slab in the graveyard. But words uttered in sincerity (he thought) never fail of some response. Though he saw his fellows leashed with a heavy chain of ignorance, stupidity, passion, and weakness, yet he divined in life some inscrutable

principle of honour and justice; some unreckon-
able essence of virtue too intimate to understand;
some fumbling aspiration toward decency, some
brave generosity of spirit, some cheerful fidelity
to Beauty. He could not see how, in a world so
obviously vast and uncouth beyond computa-
tion, they could find a puny, tidy, assumptive,
scheduled worship so satisfying. But perhaps,
since all Beauty was so staggering, it was better
they should cherish it in small formal minims.
Perhaps in this whole matter there was some
lovely symbolism that he did not understand.

The soft brightness was already lifting into
upper air, a mingled tissue of shadows lay along
the valley. In the magical clarity of the evening
light he suddenly felt (as one often does, by
unaccountable planetary instinct) that there was
a new moon. Turning, he saw it, a silver
snipping daintily afloat; and not far away, an
early star. He had found no creed in the
prayer-book that accounted for the stars. Here,
at the bottom of an ocean of sky, we look aloft
and see them thick-speckled—mere barnacles,
perhaps, on the keel of some greater ship of
space. He remembered how at home there
had been a certain burning twinkle that peeped

through the screen of the dogwood tree. As he moved on his porch, it seemed to flit to and fro, appearing and vanishing. He was often uncertain whether it was a firefly a few yards away, or a star the other side of Time. Possibly Truth was like that.

There was a light swift rustle behind him, and Miss Airedale appeared.

" Hullo! " she said. " I wondered where you were. Is this how you spend your afternoons, all alone? "

Stars, creeds, cosmologies, promptly receded into remote perspective and had to shift for themselves. It was true that Gissing had some-what avoided her lately, for he feared her fascination. He wished nothing else to interfere with his search for what he had not yet found. Postpone the female problem to the last, was his theory: not because it was insoluble, but because the solution might prove to be less interesting than the problem itself. But side by side with her, she was irresistible. A skittish brightness shone in her eyes.

" Great news! " she exclaimed. " I've per-suaded Papa to take us all down to Atlantic City for a couple of days."

" Wonderful! " cried Gissing. " Do you know, I've never been to the seashore."

" Don't worry," she replied. " I won't let you see much of the ocean. We'll go to the Traymore, and spend the whole time dancing in the Submarine Grill."

" But I must be back in time for the service on Sunday," he said.

" We're going to leave first thing in the morning. We'll go in the car, and I'll drive. Will you sit with me in the front seat? "

" Watch me! " replied Gissing gallantly.

" Come on then, or you'll be late for dinner. I'll race you home! " And she was off like a flash.

But in spite of Miss Airedale's threat, at Atlantic City they both fell into a kind of dreamy reverie. The wine-like tingle of that salty air was a quiet drug. The apparently inexhaustible sunshine was sharpened with a faint sting of coming autumn. Gissing suddenly remembered that it was ages since he had simply let his mind run slack and allowed life to go by unstudied. Mr. and Mrs. Airedale occupied a suite high up in the terraced mass of the huge hotel; they wrapped themselves in rugs and

basked on their private balcony. Gissing and
the daughter were left to their own amusements.
They bathed in the warm September surf,
they strolled the Broadwalk up beyond the old
Absecon light, where the green glimmer of
water runs in under the promenade. They sat
on the deck of the hotel—or rather Miss
Airedale sat, while Gissing, courteously
attentive, leaned over her steamer-chair. He
stood so for hours, apparently in devoted chat;
but in fact he was half in dream. The smooth
flow of the little rolling shays just below had a
soothing hypnotic effect. But it was the glorious
polished blue of the sea-horizon that bounded
all his thoughts. Even while Miss Airedale
gazed archly up at him, and he was busy with
cheerful conversation, he was conscious of that
broad band of perfect colour, monotonous,
comforting, thrilling. For the first time he
realised the great rondure of the world. His
mind went back to the section of the prayer-book
that had always touched him most pointedly—
the " Forms of Prayer to be Used at Sea." In
them he had found a note of sincere terror and
humility. And now he viewed the sea for the
first time in this setting of notable irony. The

open dazzle of placid elements, obedient only to some cosmic calculus, lay as a serene curtain against which the quaint flamboyance of the Broadwalk was all the more amusing. The clear rim of sea surfing off into space drew him with painful curiosity. Here at last was what he had needed. The proud waters went over his soul. Here indeed the blue began.

He looked down at Miss Airedale, who had gone to sleep while waiting for him to say something. He tiptoed away and went to his room to write down some ideas. Against the wide challenge of that blue hemisphere, where half the world lay open and free to the eye, the Bishop's prohibition lost weight. He was resolved to preach a sermon.

At dusk he met Miss Airedale on the high balcony that runs around the reading-room of the hotel. They were quite alone up there. Along the Broadwalk, in the pale sentimental twilight, the translucent electric globes shone like a long string of pearls. She was very tempting in a gay evening frock, and reproached him for having neglected her. She shivered a little in the cool wind coming off the darkening water. The weakness of the hour was upon

K

him. He put his arm tenderly round her as they leaned over the parapet.

"See those darling children down on the sand," she said. "I do adore puppies, don't you?"

He remembered Groups, Bunks, and Yelpers. Nothing is so potent as the love of children when you are away from them. She gazed languishing at him; he responded with a generous pressure. But his alarmed soul thrilled with panic.

"You must excuse me a moment while I dress for dinner," he said. He was strangely terrified by the look of secret understanding in her beautiful eyes. It seemed to imply some subtle, inexpressible pact. As a matter of truth, she was unconscious of it: it was only the old demiurge speaking in her—the old demiurge which was pursuing him just as ardently as he was trailing the dissolving blue of his dream. But he was much agitated as he went down in the elevator.

"Heavens," he said to himself ; "are we all only toys in the power of these terrific instincts?" For the first time he was informed of the infinite feminine capacity for being wooed.

That night they danced in the Submarine Grill. She floated in his embrace with triumphant lightness. Her eyes, utilised as temporary lamps by a lighting-circuit, of which she was quite unaware, beamed with happy lustre. The lay reader, always docile to the necessities of occasion, murmured delightful trifles. But his private thoughts were as aloof and shining and evasive as the goldfish that twinkled in the glass pool overhead. He picked up her scarf and her handkerchief when she dropped them. He smiled vaguely when she suggested that she thought she could persuade Mr. Airedale to stay in Atlantic City over the week-end, and why worry about the service on Sunday? But when she and the yawning Mrs. Airedale had retired, he hastened to his chamber and packed his bag. Stealthily he went to the desk and explained that he was leaving unexpectedly on business, and that the bill should go to Mr. Airedale, whose guest he had been. He slipped away out of the side door, and caught the late train. Mrs. Airedale chaffed her daughter that night for whining in her sleep.

# CHAPTER TWELVE

THE chapel of St. Spitz was crowded that fine Sunday morning, and the clang and thud of its bells came merrily through the thin quick air to worshippers arriving in their luxurious motors. The amiable oddity of the lay reader's demeanour as priest had added a zest to churchgoing. The congregation were particularly pleased, on this occasion, to see Gissing appear in surplice and stole. They had felt that his attire on the previous Sundays had been a little too informal. And when, at the time usually allotted to the sermon, Gissing climbed the pulpit steps, unfurled a sheaf of manuscript, and gazed solemnly about, they settled back into the pew cushions in a comfortable, receptive mood. They had a subconscious feeling that if their souls were to be saved, it was better to have it done with all the proper formalities. They did not notice that he was rather pale, and that his nose twitched nervously.

"My friends," he said, "in this beautiful

little chapel, on this airy hilltop, one might, if anywhere, speak with complete honesty. For you who gather here for worship are, in the main, people of great affairs; accustomed to looking at life with high spirit and with quick imagination. I will ask you then to be patient with me while I exhort you to carry into your religion the same enterprising and ambitious gusto that has made worldly careers a success. You are accustomed to deal with great affairs. Let me talk to you about the Great Affairs of God."

Gissing had been far too agitated to be able to recognise any particular members of his audience. All the faces were fused into a common blur. Miss Airedale, he knew, was in the organ loft, but he had not seen her since his flight from Atlantic City, for he had removed from the Airedale mansion before her return, and had made himself a bed in the corner of the vestry-room. He feared she was angry: there had been a vigorous growling note in some of the bass pipes of the organ as she played the opening hymn. He had not seen a tall white-haired figure who came into the chapel rather late, after the service had begun, and took a seat at the back. Bishop Borzoi had seized the opportunity to drive out to Dalmatian Heights this morning to see how his protege was getting on. When the Bishop saw his lay reader appear in surplice and scarlet hood, he was startled. But when the amateur parson actually ascended the pulpit, the Bishop's face was a study. The hair on the back of his neck bristled slightly.

" It is so easy," Gissing continued, " to let life go by us in its swift amusing course, that sometimes it hardly seems worth while to attempt any bold strokes for truth. Truth, of course, does not need our assistance; it can afford to ignore our errors. But in this quiet place, among the whisper of the trees, I seem to have heard a disconcerting sound. I have heard laughter, and I think it is the laughter of God."

The congregation stirred a little, with polite uneasiness. This was not quite the sort of thing to which they were accustomed.

" Why should God laugh? " I think it is because He sees very often, when we pretend to be worshipping Him, we are really worshipping and gratifying ourselves. I used the phrase ' Great Affairs.' The point I want to make is that God deals with far greater affairs than we have realised. We have imagined Him on too petty a scale. If God is so great, we must approach Him in a spirit of greatness. He is not interested in trivialities—trivialities of ritual, of creed, of ceremony. We have imagined a vain thing—a God of our own species; merely adding to the conception, to gild and consecrate, a futile fuzbuz of supernaturalism. My friends, the God I imagine is something more than a formula on Sundays and an oath during the week."

Those sitting in the rear of the Chapel were startled to hear a low rumbling sound proceeding from the diaphragm of the Bishop, who half rose from his seat and then, by a great effort of will, contained himself. But Gissing, rapt in his honourable speculations, continued with growing happiness.

" I ask you, though probably in vain, to lay aside for the moment your inherited timidities and conventions. I ask you to lay aside pride, which is the devil itself and the cause of most unhappiness. I ask you to rise to the height of a great conception. To ' magnify ' God is a common phrase in our observances. Then let us truly magnify Him—not minify, as the theologians do. If God is anything more than a social fetish, then He must be so much more that He includes, and explains everything. It may sound inconceivable to you, it may sound sacrilegious, but I suggest to you that it is even possible God may be a biped——"

The Bishop could restrain himself no longer. He rose with flaming eyes and stood in the aisle. Mr. Airedale, Mr. Dobermann-Pinscher, and several other prominent members of the Church burst into threatening growls. A wild bark and clamour broke from Mr. Towser, the Sunday School superintendent, and his pupils, who sat in the little gallery over the door. And then, to Gissing's horror and amazement, Mr. Poodle appeared from behind a pillar where he had been chafing unseen. In a fierce tenor voice shaken with indignation he cried:

" Heretic and hypocrite! Pay no attention to his abominable nonsense! He deserted his family to lead a life of pleasure! "

" Seize him! " cried the Bishop in a voice of thunder.

The church was now in an uproar. A shrill yapping sounded among the choir. Mrs. Airedale swooned; the Bishop's progress up the

aisle was impeded by a number of ladies hastening for an exit. Old Mr. Dingo, the sexton,
seized the bell-rope in the porch and set up a
furious pealing. Cries of rage mingled with
hysterical howls from the ladies. Gissing,
trembling with horror, surveyed the atrocious
hubbub. But it was high time to move, or his
retreat would be cut off. He abandoned his
manuscript and bounded down the pulpit stairs.

" Unfrock him! " yelled Mr. Poodle.

" He's never been frocked! " roared the
Bishop.

" Imposter! " cried Mr. Airedale.

" Excommunicate him! " screamed Mr.
Towser.

" Take him before the consistory ! " shouted
Mr. Poodle.

Gissing started toward the vestry door, but
was delayed by the mass of scuffling choir-
puppies who had seized this uncomprehended
diversion as a chance to settle some scores of
their own. The clamour was maddening. The
Bishop leapt the chancel rail and was about to
seize him when Miss Airedale, loyal to the last,
interposed. She flung herself upon the Bishop.

" Run, run! " she cried. " They'll kill you! "

Gissing profited by this assistance. He pushed over the lectern upon Mr. Poodle, who was clutching at his surplice. He checked Mr. Airedale by hurling little Tommy Bull, one of the choir, bodily at him. Tommy's teeth fastened automatically upon Mr. Airedale's ear. The surplice, which Mr. Poodle was still holding, parted with a rip, and Gissing was free. With a yell of defiance he tore through the vestry and round behind the chapel.

He could not help pausing a moment to scan the amazing scene, which had been all Sabbath calm a few moments before. From the long line of motor-cars parked outside the chapel incredible chaffeurs were leaping, hurrying to see what had happened. The shady grove shook with the hideous clamour of the bell, still wildly tolled by the frantic sexton Then sudden excitement had liberated private quarrels long decently repressed: in the porch Mrs. Retriever and Mrs. Dobermann-Pinscher were locked in combat. With a splintering crash one of the choir-pups came sailing through a stained glass window, evidently thrown by some infuriated adult. He recognised the voice of Mr. Towser, raised in vigorous lamentation. To judge by the sound, Mr. Towser's pupils had turned upon him and were giving him a bad time. Above all he could hear the clear war-cry of Miss Airedale and the embittered yells of Mr. Poodle. Then from the quaking edifice burst Bishop Borzoi, foaming with wrath, his clothes much tattered, and followed by Mr. Poodle, Mr. Airedale, and several others. They cast about for a moment, and then the Bishop saw him. With a joint halloo they launched toward him.

There was no time to lose. He fled down the shady path between the trees, but with a hopeless horror in his heart. He could not long outdistance such a runner as the Bishop, whose tremendous strides would surely overhaul him in the end. If only he had known how to drive a car, he might have commandeered one of the long row waiting by the gate. But he was no motorist. Miss Airedale could have saved him, in her racing roadster, but she had not emerged from the mêlée in the chapel. Perhaps the Bishop had bitten her. His blood warmed with anger.

It happened that they had been mending the county highways, and a large steam-roller stood a few hundred feet down the road, drawn up beside the ditch. Gissing knew that it was customary to leave these engines with the fire banked and a gentle pressure of steam simmering in the boiler. It was his only chance, and he seized it. But to his dismay, when he reached the machine, which lay just round a bend in the road, he found it shrouded with a huge tarpaulin. However, this suggested a desperate chance. He whipped nimbly inside the covering and hid in the coal-box. Lying there, he heard the chase go panting by.

As soon as he dared, he climbed out, stripped off the canvas, and gazed at the bulky engine. It was one of those very tall and impressive rollers with a canopy over the top. The machinery was not complicated, and the ingenuity of desperation spurred him on. Hurriedly he opened the draughts in the fire-box, shook up the coals, and saw the needle begin to quiver on the pressure-guage. He experimented with one or two levers and handles. The first one he touched let off a loud scream from the whistle. Then he discovered the throttle. He opened it a few notches cautiously. The ponderous machine, with a horrible clanking and grinding, began to move forward.

A steam-roller may seem the least helpful of all vehicles in which to conduct an urgent flight; but Gissing's reasoning was sound. In the first place, no one would expect to find a hunted fugitive in this lumbering, sluggish behemoth of the road. Secondly, sitting perched high up in the driving saddle, right under the canopy, he was not easily seen by the casual passer-by. And thirdly, if the pursuit came to close grips, he was still in a stragetic position. For this, the most versatile of all land-machines except the military tank, can move across fields, crash through underbush, and travel in a hundred places that would stall a motor car. He rumbled off down the road somewhat exhilarated. He found the scarlet stole twisted round his neck, and tied it to one of the stanchions of the canopy as a flag of defiance.

It was not long before he saw the posse of pursuit returning along the road, very hot and angry. He crunched along solemnly, busying himself to get up a strong head of steam. There they were, the Bishop, Mr. Poodle, Mr. Airedale, Mr. Dobermann-Pinscher, and Mr.

Towser. Mr. Poodle was talking excitedly: the Bishop's tongue ran in and out over his gleaming teeth. He was not saying much, but his manner was full of deadly wrath. They paid no attention to the roller, and were about to pass it without even looking up, when Gissing, in a sudden fit of indignation, gave the wheel a quick twirl and turned his clumsy engine upon them. They escaped only by a hair's breadth from being flattened out like pastry. Then the Bishop, looking up, recognised the renegade. With a cry of anger they all leaped at the roller.

But he was so high above them, they had no chance. He seized the coal-scoop and whanged Mr. Poodle across the skull. The Bishop came dangerously near reaching him, but Gissing released a jet of scalding steam from an exhaust-cock, which gave the impetuous prelate much cause for grief. A lump of coal, accurately thrown, discouraged Mr. Airedale. Mr. Towser, attacking on the other side of the engine, managed to scramble up so high that he carried away the embroidered stole, but otherwise the fugitive had all the best of it. Mr. Dobermann-Pinscher burned his feet trying to climb up the side of the boiler. From the summit of his uncouth vehicle Gissing looked down undismayed.

" Miserable freethinker! " said Borzoi. " You shall be tried by the assembly of Bishops."

" In a mere lay reader," quoted Gissing, " a slight laxity is allowable. You had better go back and calm down the congregation, or they'll tear the chapel to bits. This kind of thing will have a very bad influence on church discipline."

They shouted additional menace, but Gissing had already started his deafening machinery and could not hear what was said. He left them bickering by the roadside.

For fear of further pursuit, he turned off the highway a little beyond, and rumbled noisily down a rustic lane between high banks and hedges where sumac was turning red. Strangely enough, there was something very comforting about his enormous crawling contraption. It was docile and reliable, like an elephant. The crashing clangour of its movement was soon forgotten—became, in fact, an actual stimulus to thought. For the mere pleasure of novelty, he steered through a copse, and took joy in seeing the monster crash through thickets and brambles, and then across a field of crackling stubble. Steering toward the lonelier regions of that farming country, presently he halted in a dingle of birches beside a small pond. He spent some time very happily, carefully studying the machinery. He found some waste and an oil-can in the tool-chest, and polished until the metal shone. The water looked rather low in the gauge, and he replenished it from the pool.

It was while grooming the roller that it struck him his own appearance was unusual for a high-way mechanic. He was still wearing the famous floorwalker suit, which he had punctiliously donned every Sunday for chapel. But he had had to flee without a hat—even without his luggage, which was neatly packed in a bag in the vestry. That, he felt sure, Mr. Poodle had already burst open for evidences of heresy and schism. The pearly trousers were stained with oil and coal-dust; the neat cutaway coat bore smears of engine-grease. As long as he stuck to the roller and the telltale garments, pursuit and identification would of course be easy enough. But he had taken a fancy to the machine : he decided not to abandon it yet.

Obviously, it was better to keep to the roads, where the engine would at any rate be less surprisingly conspicuous, and where it would leave no trail. So he made a long curcuit across meadows and pastures, carrying a devilish clamour into the quiet Sunday afternoon. Regaining a macadam surface, he set off at random, causing considerable annoyance to the motoring public. Finding that his cutaway coat caused jeers and merriment, he removed it; and when anyone showed a disposition to inquire, he explained that he was doing penance for an ill-judged wager. His oscillating perch above the boiler was extraordinarily warm, and he bought a gallon jug of cider from a farmer by the way. Cheering himself with this, and reviewing in his mind the queer experiences of the past months, he went thundering mildly on.

At first he had feared a furious pursuit on the part of the Bishop, or even a whole college of bishops, quickly mobilised for the event. He had imagined them speeding after him in a huge motor-bus, and himself keeping them at bay with lumps of coal. But gradually he realised that the Bishop would not further jeopardize his dignity, or run the risk of making himself ridiculous. Mr. Poodle would undoubtedly set the township road commissioner on his trail, and

L

he would be liable to seizure for the theft of a steam-roller. But that could hardly happen so quickly. In the meantime, a plan had been forming in his mind, but it would require darkness for its execution.

Darkness did not delay in coming. As he jolted cheerfully from road to road, holding up long strings of motors at every corner while he jovially held out his arm as a sign that he was going to turn, dark purple clouds were massing and piling up. Foreseeing a storm, he bought some provisions at a roadhouse, and turned into a field, where he camped in the lee of a forest of birches. He cooked himself an excellent supper, toasting bread and frankfurters in the fire-box of the roller. With boiling water from a steam-cock he brewed a panikin of tea; and sat placidly admiring the fawn-pink light on wide pampas of bronze grasses, tawny as a panther's hide. A strong wind began to draw from the south-east He lit the lantern at the rear of the machine, and by the time the rain came hissing upon the hot boiler, he was ready. Luckily he had saved the tarpaulin. He spread this on the ground underneath the roller, and curled up in it. The glow from the fire-box kept him warm and dry.

" Summer is over," he said to himself, as he heard the clash and spouting of rain all about him. He lay for some time, not sleepy, thinking theology, and enjoying the close tumult of wind and weather.

People who have had an arm or a leg amputated, he reflected, say they can still feel pains in the absent member. Well, there's an analogy in that. Modern scepticism has amputated God from the heart; but there is still a twinge where the arteries were sewn up.

He slept peacefully until about two in the morning, except when a red-hot coal, slipping through the grate-bars, burned a lamentable hole in his trousers. When he woke, the night still dripped, but was clear aloft. He started the engine and drove cautiously, along black slippery roads, to Mr. Poodle's house. In spite of the unavoidable racket, no one stirred: he surmised that the curate slept soundly after the crises of the day. He left the engine by the doorstep, pinning a note to the steering wheel. It said:

TO REV. J. ROVER POODLE

this useful steam-roller

as a symbol of the theological mind

MR. GISSING

# CHAPTER THIRTEEN

THE steamship *Pomerania*, which had sailed at noon, was a few hours out of port on a calm grey sea. The passengers, after the bustle of lunch and arranging their staterooms, had settled into their deck chairs and were telling each other how much they loved the ocean. Captain Scottie had taken his afternoon constitutional on his private strip of starboard deck just aft the bridge, and was sitting in his comfortable cabin expecting a cup of tea. He was a fine old sea-dog—squat, grizzled, severe, with wiry eyebrows, a short coarse beard, and watchful quick eyes. A characteristic Scot, beneath his reticent, conscientious dignity there was abundant humour and affection. He would have been recognised anywhere as a sailor: those short, solid legs were perfectly adapted for balancing on a rolling deck. He stood by habit as though he were leaning into a stiff gale. His mouth always held a pipe, which he smoked in short, brisk whiffs, as though expecting to be interrupted at any moment by an iceberg.

The steward brought in the tea-tray, and Captain Scottie settled into his large armchair to enjoy it. His eye glanced automatically at the barometer.

"A little wind to-night," he said, his nose wrinkling unconsciously as the cover was lifted from the hot dish of anchovy toast.

"Yes, sir," said the steward, but lingered, apparently anxious to speak further.

"Well, Shepherd?"

"Beg pardon, sir, but the Chief Steward wanted me to say they've found someone stowed away in the linen locker, sir. Queer kind of fellow, sir, talks a bit like a padre. 'E must've come aboard by the engine-room gangway, sir, and climbed into that locker near the barber shop."

The problem of stowaways is familiar enough to shipmasters. "Send him up to me," said the Captain.

A few minutes later Gissing appeared, escorted by a burly quartermaster. Even the experienced Captain admitted to himself that this was something new in the category of stow-aways. Never before had he seen one in a braided cutaway coat and wedding trousers. It was true that the garments were in grievous condition, but they were worn with an air. The stowaway's face showed some embarrassment, but not at all the usual hangdog mien of such wastrels. Involuntarily his tongue moistened when he saw the tray of tea (for he had not eaten since his supper on the steam-roller the night before), but he kept his eyes politely averted from the food. They rose to a white-painted girder that ran athwart the cabin ceiling. CERTIFIED TO ACCOMMODATE THE MASTER he read there, in letters deeply incised into the thick paint. "A good Christian ship," he said to himself. "It sounds like the Y.M.C.A." He was pleased to think that his suspicion was already confirmed : ships were more religious than anything on land.

The Captain dismissed the quartermaster, and addressed himself sternly to the culprit.

"Well, what have you to say for yourself? "

"Please, Captain," said Gissing politely, " do not allow your tea to get cold. I can talk while you eat."

Behind his grim demeanour the Captain was very near to smiling at this naïveté. No Briton is wholly implacable at tea-time, and he felt a genuine curiosity about this unusual offender.

" What was your idea in coming aboard? " he said. " Do you know that I can put you in irons until we get across, and then have you sent home for punishment? I suppose it's the old story: You want to go sight-seeing on the other side? "

" No, Captain," said Gissing. " I have come to sea to study theology."

In spite of himself the Captain was touched by this amazing statement. He was a Scot, as we have said. He poured a cup of tea to conceal his astonishment.

" Theology! " he exclaimed. " The theology of hard work is what you will find most of aboard ship. Carry on and do your duty; keep a sharp lookout, all gear shipshape, salute the bridge when going on watch, that is the whole duty of a good officer. That's plenty theology for a seaman." But the skipper's eye turned brightly toward his bookshelves, where he had several volumes of sermons, mostly of a Calvinist sort.

" I am not afraid of work," said Gissing.

" But I'm looking for horizons. In my work ashore I never could find any."

" Your horizon is likely to be peeling potatoes in the galley," remarked the Captain. " I understand they are short-handed there. Or sweeping our bunks in the steerage. Ethics of the dust! What would you say to that? "

" Sir," replied Gissing, " I shall be grateful for any task, however menial, that permits me to meditate. I understand your point of view. By coming aboard your ship I have broken the law, I have committed a crime; but not a sin. Crime and sin, every theologian admits, are not co-extensive."

The Captain sailed head-on into argument.

" What? " he cried. " Are you aware of the doctrine of Moral Inability in a Fallen State? Sit down, sit down, and have a cup of tea. We must discuss this."

He rang for the steward and ordered an extra cup and a fresh supply of toast. At that moment Gissing heard two quick strokes of a bell, rung somewhere forward—a clear, musical, melancholy tone, echoed promptly in other parts of the ship.

"What is that, Captain?" he asked anxiously. "An accident?"

"Two bells in the first dog-watch," said the Captain. "I fear you are as much a lubber at sea as you are in theology."

The next two hours passed like a flash. Gissing found the skipper, in spite of his occasional moods of austerity, a delicious companion. They discussed Theosophy, Spiritualism, and Christian Science, all of which the Captain, with sturdy but rather troubled vehemence, linked with Primitive Magic. Gissing, seeing that his only hope of establishing himself in the sailor's regard was to disagree and keep the argument going, plunged into psycho-analysis and the philosophy of the unconscious. Rather unwarily he ventured to introduce a nautical illustration into the talk.

"Your compass needle," he said, "points to the North Pole, and although it has never been to the Pole, and cannot even concieve of it, yet it testifies irresistibly to the existence of such a place."

"I trust you navigate your soul more skilfully than you would navigate this vessel," retorted the Captain. "In the first place, the needle does not point to the North Pole at all, but to the magnetic pole. Furthermore, it has to be adjusted by magnets to counteract deviation. Mr. Gissing, you may be a sincere student of theology, but you have not allowed for your own temperamental deviation. Why, even the gyro compass has to be adjusted for latitude error. You landsmen think that a ship is simply a floating hotel. I should like to have the Bishop you spoke of study a little navigation. That would put into him a healthy respect for the marvels of science. On board ship, sir, the binnacle is kept locked and the key is on the watch-chain of the master. It should be so in all intellectual matters. Confide them to those capable of understanding."

Gissing saw that the Captain greatly relished his sense of superiority, so he made a remark of intentional simplicity.

" The binnacle? " he said. " I thought that was the little shellfish that clings to the bottom of the boat? "

" Don't you dare call my ship a *boat!* " said the Captain. " At sea, a boat means only a life-boat or some other small vagabond craft. Come out on the bridge and I'll show you a thing or two."

The evening had closed in hazy, and the *Pomerania* swung steadily in a long plunging roll. At the weather wing of the bridge, gazing sharply over the canvas dodger, was Mr. Pointer, the vigilant Chief Officer, peering off rigidly as though mesmerised, but saying nothing. He gave the Captain a corteous salute, but kept silence. At the large mahogany wheel, gently steadying it to the quarterly roll of the sea, stood Dane, a tall, solemn quartermaster. In spite of a little uneasiness, due to the unfamiliar motion, Gissing was greatly elated by the wheelhouse, which seemed even more thrillingly romantic than any pulpit. Uncomprehendingly, but with admiration, he examined the binnacle, the engine-room telegraphs, the telephones, the rack of signal-flags, the buttons for closing bulkheads, and the rotating clearview screen for lookout in thick weather. Aloft he could see the masthead light, gently soaring in slow arcs.

" I'll show you my particular pride," said the Captain, evidently pleased by his visitor's delighted enthusiasm.

Gissing wondered what ingenious device of science this might be.

Captain Scottie stepped to the weather gunwale of the bridge. He pointed to the smoke, which was rolling rapidly from the funnels.

"You see," he said, "there's quite a strong breeze blowing. But look here."

He lit a match and held it unshielded above the canvas screen which was lashed along the front of the bridge. To Gissing's surprise it burned steadily without blowing out.

"I've invented a convex wind-shield which splits the air just forward of the bridge. I can stand here and light my pipe in the stiffest gale, without any trouble."

On the decks below Gissing heard a bugle blowing gaily, a bright persuasive sound.

"Six bells," the Captain said. "I must dress for dinner. Before I start you potato-peeling, I should like to clear up that little discussion of ours about Free Will. One or two things you said interested me."

He paced the bridge for a minute, thinking hard.

"I'll test your sincerity," he said. "To-night you can bunk in the chart-room. I'll have some dinner sent up to you. I wish you would write me an essay of say, two thousand words on the subject of ' Necessity.' "

For a moment Gissing pondered whether it would not be better to be put in irons and rationed with bread and water. The wind was freshening, and the *Pomerania's* sharp bow slid heavily into broad hills of sea, crashing them into crumbling rollers of suds which fell outward and hissed along her steep sides. The silent Mr. Pointer escorted him into the chartroom—a bare, business-like place, with a large table, a map-cabinet, and a settee. Here, presently, a steward appeared with excellent viands, and a pen, ink, and notepaper. After a cautious meal, Gissing felt more comfortable. There is something about a wet, windy evening at sea that turns the mind naturally toward metaphysics. He pushed away the dishes and began to write.

Later in the evening the Captain reappeared. He looked pleased when he saw a number of sheets already covered with script.

" Rum lot of passengers this trip," he said. " I don't seem to see any who look interesting. All Big Business and that sort of thing. I must say it's nice to have someone who can talk about books, and so on, once in a while."

Gissing realised that sometimes a shipmaster's life must be a lonely one. The weight of responsibility is always upon him; etiquette prevents his becoming familiar with his officers; small wonder if he pines occasionally for a little congenial talk to relieve his mind.

" Big Business, did you say? " Gissing remarked. " Ah, I could write you quite an essay about that. I used to be General Manager of Beagle and Company."

" Come into my cabin and have a liqueur," said the skipper. " Let the essay go until to-morrow."

The Captain turned on the electric stove in his cabin, for the night was cold. It was a snug sanctum: at the portholes were little chintz curtains; over the bunk was a convenient reading lamp. On the wall a brass pendulum swung slowly, registering the roll of the ship. The ruddy shine of the stove lit up the orderly desk and the photographs of the Captain's family.

" Yours? " said Gissing, looking at a group of three puppies with droll Scottish faces.

" Aye," said the Captain.

" I've three of my own," said Gissing, with a private pang of homesickness. The skipper's cosy quarters were the most truly domestic he had seen since the evening he first fled from responsibility.

Captain Scottie was surprised. Certainly this eccentric stranger in the badly-damaged wedding garments had not given the impression of a family head. Just then the steward entered with a decanter of benedictine and small glasses.

" Braw days and bonny! " said the Captain, raising his crystal.

" Secure amidst perils! " replied Gissing courteously. It was the phrase engraved upon the ship's notepaper, on which he had been writing. and it had impressed itself on his mind.

" You said you had been a General Manager."

Gissing told, with some vivacity, of his experiences in the world of trade. The Captain poured another small liqueur.

" They're fine halesome liquor," he said.

" Sincerely yours," said Gissing, nodding over the glass. He was beginning to feel quite at home in the navigating quarters of the ship,

and hoped the potato-peeling might be postponed as long as possible.

" How far had you gone in your essay? "
asked the Captain.

" Not very far, I fear.  I was beginning by
laying down a few psychological fundamentals."

" Excellent!   Will you read it to me? "

Gissing went to get his manuscript, and read
it aloud.  The Captain listened attentively, puff-
ing clouds of smoke.

" I am sorry this is such a short voyage," he
said when Gissing finished.  " You have ap-
roached the matter from an entirely naïf and
instinctive standpoint, and it will take some time
to show you your errors.  Before I demolish
your arguments I should like to turn them over
in my mind.  I will reduce my ideas to writing
and then read them to you."

" I should like nothing better," said Gissing.
" And I can think over the subject more carefully while I peel the potatoes."

" Nonsense," said the Captain.  " I do not
often get a chance to discuss theology. I will tell
you my idea.  You spoke of your experience as
General Manager, when you had charge of a
thousand employees.  One of the things we

need on this ship is a staff-captain, to take over the management of the personnel. That would permit me to concentrate entirely on navigation. In a vessel of this size it is wrong that the master should have to carry the entire responsibility."

He rang for the steward.

" My compliments to Mr. Pointer, and tell him to come here."

Mr. Pointer appeared shortly in oilskins, saluted, and gazed fixedly at his superior, with one foot raised upon the brass door-sill.

" Mr. Pointer," said Captain Scottie, " I have appointed Captain Gissing staff-captain. Take orders from him as you would from me. He will have complete charge of the ship's discipline."

" Aye, aye, sir," said Mr. Pointer, and stood a moment intently to see if there were further orders, saluted again, and withdrew.

" Now you had better turn in," said the skipper. " Of course you must wear uniform. I'll send the tailor up to you at once. He can remodel one of my suits overnight. The trousers will have to be lengthened."

On the chart-room sofa, Gissing dozed and waked and dozed again. On the bridge near by

M

he heard the steady tread of feet, the mysterious words of the officer on watch passing the course to his relief. Bells rang with sharp double clang. Through the open port he could hear the alternate boom and hiss of the sea under the bows. With the stately lift and lean of the ship there mingled a faint driving vibration.

# CHAPTER FOURTEEN

THE first morning in any new environment is always the most exciting. Gissing was already awake, and watching the novel sight of a patch of sunshine sliding to and fro on the deck of the chart-room, when there was a gentle tap on the door. The Captain's steward entered, carrying a handsome uniform.

" Six bells, sir," he said. " Your bath is laid on."

Gissing was not very sure just what time it was, but the steward held out a dressing-gown for him to slip on, so he took the hint, and followed him to the Captain's private bathroom, where he plunged gaily into warm salt water. He was hardly dressed before breakfast was laid for him in the chart-room. It was a breakfast greatly to his liking—porridge, scrambled eggs, grilled kidneys and bacon, coffee, toast, and marmalade. Evidently the hardships of sea life had been greatly exaggerated by fiction writers.

He was a trifle bashful about appearing on the bridge in his blue and brass formality, and waited a while, thinking Captain Scottie might come. But no one disturbed him, so bye and bye he went out. It was a brisk morning with a fresh breeze and plenty of white caps. Dancing rainbows hovered about the bow when an occasional explosion of spray burst up into the sunlight. Mr. Pointer was on the bridge, still gazing steadily into the distance. He saluted Gissing, but said nothing. The quartermaster at the wheel also saluted in silence. A seaman wiping down the paintwork on the deckhouse saluted. Gissing returned these gestures punctiliously, and began to pace the bridge from side to side. He soon grew accustomed to the varying slant of the deck, and felt that his footing showed a nautical assurance.

Now, for the first time, he enjoyed an untrammelled horizon on all sides. The sea, he observed, was not really blue—not at any rate the blue he had supposed. Where it seethed flatly along the hull, laced with swirls of milky foam, it was almost black. Farther away, it was green, or darkly violet. A ladder led to the top of the charthouse, and from this commanding height the whole body of the ship lay below him. How alive she seemed, how full of personality! The strong funnels, the tall masts that moved so delicately against the pale open sky, the distant stern that now dipped low in a comfortable hollow, and now soared and threshed onward with a swimming thrust, the whole vital organism spoke to the eye and the imagination. In the centre of this vast circle she moved, royal and serene. She was more beautiful than the element she rode on, for perhaps there was something meaningless in that pure vacant round of sea and sky. Once its immense azure was grasped and noted, it brought nothing to the mind. Reason was indignant to conceive it, sloping endlessly away.

The placid, beautifully-planned routine of shipboard passed on its accustomed course, and he began to suspect that his staff-captaincy was a sinecure. Down below he could see the passengers briskly promenading, or drowsing under their rugs. On the hurricane deck, aft, a sailor was chalking a shuffleboard court. It occurred to him that all this might become monotonous unless he found some actual part in it. Just then Captain Scottie appeared on the bridge, took a quick look round, and joined him on top of the charthouse.

"Good morning!" he said. "You won't think me rude if you don't see much of me? Thinking about those ideas of yours, I have come upon some rather puzzling stuff. I must work the whole thing out more clearly. Your suggestion that Conscience points the way to an integration of personality into a higher type of divinity, seems to me off the track; but I haven't quite downed it yet. I'm going to shut myself up to-day and consider the matter. I leave you in charge."

"I shall be perfectly happy," said Gissing. "Please don't worry about me."

"You suggest that all the conditions of life at sea, our mastery of the forces of Nature, and so on, seem to show that we have perfect freedom of will, and adapt everything to our desires. I believe just the contrary. The forces of Nature compel us to approach them in their own way, otherwise we are shipwrecked. It is in the conditions of Nature that this ship should reach port in eight days, otherwise we should get nowhere. We do it because it is our destiny."

"I am not so sure of that," said Gissing. But

the Captain had already departed with a clouded brow.

On the chart-room roof Gissing had discovered an alluring instrument, the exact use of which he did not know. It seemed to be some kind of steering control. The dial was lettered, from left to right, as follows:—HARD A PORT, PORT, STEADY, COURSE, STEADY, STARBD., HARD A STARBD. At present the handle stood upon the section marked COURSE. After a careful study of the whole sea-scape, it seemed to Gissing that off to the south the ocean looked more blue and more interesting. After some hesitation he moved the handle to the PORT mark, and waited to see what would happen. To his delight he saw the bow swing slowly round, and the *Pomerania's* gleaming wake spread behind her in a whitened curve. He descended to the bridge, a little nervous as to what Mr. Pointer might say, but he found the Mate gazing across the water with the same fierce and unwearying attention.

" I have changed the course," he said.

Mr. Pointer saluted, but said nothing.

Having succeeded so far, Gissing ventured upon another innovation. He had been greatly tempted by the wheel, and envied the stolid quartermaster who was steering. So, assuming an air of calm certainty, he entered the wheel-house.

"I'll take her for a while," he said.

"Aye, aye, sir," said the quartermaster, and surrendered the wheel to him.

"You might string out a few flags," Gissing said. He had been noticing the bright signal buntings in the rack, and thought it a pity not to use them.

"I like to see a ship well dressed," he added.

"Aye, aye, sir," said Dane. "Any choice, sir?"

Gissing picked out a string of flags which were particularly lively in colour-scheme, and had them hoisted. Then he gave his attention to the wheel. He found it quite an art, and was surprised to learn that a big ship requires so much helm. But it was very pleasant. He took care to steer toward patches of sea that looked interesting, and to cut into any particular waves that took his fancy. After an hour or so, he sighted a fishing schooner, and gave chase. He found it so much fun to run close beside her (taking care to pass to leeward, so as not to cut off her wind) that a mile farther on he turned and steered a neat circle about the bewildered craft. The *Pomerania's* passengers were greatly interested, and lined the rails trying to make out what the fishermen were shouting. The captain of the schooner seemed particularly agitated, kept waving at the signal flags and barking through a megaphone. During these manœuvres Mr. Pointer gazed so hard at the horizon that Gissing felt a bit embarrassed.

" I thought it wise to find out exactly what our turning-circle is," he said.

Mr. Pointer saluted. He was a well-trained officer.

Late in the afternoon the Captain reappeared, looking more cheerful. Gissing was still at the helm, which he found so fascinating, he would not relinquish it. He had ordered his tea served on a little stand beside the wheel, so that he could drink while he steered.

" Hullo! " said the Captain. " I see you've changed the course."

" It seemed best to do so," said Gissing firmly. He felt that to show any weakness at this point would be fatal.

" Oh, well, probably it doesn't matter. I'm coming round to some of your ideas."

Gissing saw that this would never do. Unless he could keep the master disturbed by philosophic doubts, Scottie would expect to resume command of the ship.

" Well," he said, " I've been thinking about it, too. I believe I went a bit too far. But what do you think about this? Do you believe that Conscience is inherited or acquired? You see how important that is. If Conscience is a kind of automatic oracle, infallible and perfect, what becomes of free will ? And if, on the other hand, Conscience is only a laboriously-trained perception of moral and social utilities, where does your deity come in? "

Gissing was aware that this dilemma would not hold water for very long, and was painfully impromptu; but it hit the Captain amidships.

" By Jove," he said, " that's terrible, isn't it? It's no use trying to carry on until I've got that under the hatch. Look here, would you mind, just as a favour, keep things going while I wrestle with that question?—I know it's asking a lot, but perhaps———"

" It's quite all right," Gissing replied. " Naturally you want to work these things out."

The Captain started to leave the bridge, but by old-seafaring habit he cast a keen glance at the sky. He saw the bright string of code flags fluttering. He seemed startled.

" Are you signalling any one? " he asked.

" No one in particular. I thought it looked better to have a few flags about."

" I daresay you're right. But better take them down if you speak a ship. They're rather confusing."

" Confusing? I thought they were just to brighten things up."

" You have two different signals up. They read, *Bubonic plague, give me a wide berth. Am coming to your assistance.*"

Toward dinner time, when Gissing had left the wheel and was humming a tune as he walked the bridge, the steward came to him.

" The Captain's compliments, sir, and would you take his place in the saloon to-night? He says he's very busy writing, sir, and would take it as a favour."

Gissing was always obliging. There was just a hint of conscious sternness in his manner as he

entered the *Pomerania's* beautiful dining saloon,
for he wished the passengers to realise that their
lives depended upon his prudence and sea-lore.
Twice during the meal he instructed the steward
to bring him the latest barometer reading; and
after the desert he scribbled a note on the back
of a menu-card and had it sent to the Chief
Engineer.   It said:—

Dear Chief: Please keep up a good head of steam
to-night.   I am expecting dirty weather.

> MR. GISSING,
> (Staff-Captain)

What the Chief said when he received the
message is not included in the story.

But the same social aplomb that had made
Gissing successful as a floorwalker now came
to his rescue as mariner.   The passengers at
the Captain's table were amazed at his genial
charm.   His anecdotes of sea life were heartily
applauded  After dinner he circulated gracefully
applauded.   After dinner he circulated gracefully in the ladies lounge, and took coffee there
surrounded by a chattering bevy.   He organised a
little impromptu concert in the music room, and
when that was well started, slipped away to the

smoke-room. Here he found a pool being organised as to the exact day and hour when the
*Pomerania* would reach port. Appealed to for
his opinion, he advised caution. On all sides he
was in demand, for dancing, for bridge, for a
recitation. At length he slipped away, pleading
that he must keep himself fit in case of fog. The
passengers were loud in his praise, asserting that
they had never met so agreeable a sea-captain.
One elderly lady said she remembered crossing
with him in the old *Caninia*, years ago, and that
he was just the same then.

# CHAPTER FIFTEEN

A ND so the voyage went on. Gissing was
quite content to do a two-hour trick at
the wheel both morning and afternoon,
and worked out some new principles of steering
which gave him pleasure. In the first place, he
noticed that the shuffle-board and quoit players,
on the boat deck aft, were occasionally annoyed
by cinders from the stacks, so he made it a general plan to steer so that the smoke blew at right
angles to the ship's course. As the wind was
prevailingly west, this meant that his general
trend was southerly. Whenever he saw another
vessel, a mass of floating sea-weed, a porpoise,
or even a sea-gull, he steered directly for it, and
passed as close as possible, to have a good look
at it. Even Mr. Pointer admitted (in the mates'
mess) that he had never experienced so eventful
a voyage. To keep the quartermasters from
being idle, Gissing had them knit him a rope
hammock to be slung in the chart-room. He

felt that this would be more nautical than a plush settee.

There was a marvellous sense of power in standing at the wheel and feeling the great hull reply to his touch. Occasionally Captain Scottie would emerge from his cabin, look round with a faint surprise, and come to the bridge to see what was happening. Mr. Pointer would salute mutely, and continue to study the skyline with indignant absorption. The Captain would approach the wheel, where Gissing was deep in thought. Rubbing his hands, the Captain would say heartily, " Well, I think I've got it all clear now."

Gissing sighed.

" What is it?" the Captain inquired anxiously.

" I'm bothered about the subconscious. They tell us nowadays that it's the subconscious mind that is really important. The more mental operations we can turn over to the subconscious realm, the happier we will be, and the more efficient. Morality, theology, and everything really worth while, as I understand it, spring from the subconscious."

The Captain's look of cheer would vanish.

" Maybe there's something in that."

"If so," Gissing continued, "then perhaps consciousness is entirely spurious. It seems to me that before we can get anywhere at all, we've got to draw the line between the conscious and the subconscious. What bothers me is, am I conscious of having a subconscious or not? Sometimes I think I am, and then again I'm doubtful. But if I'm aware of my subconscious, then it isn't a genuine subconscious, and the whole thing's just another delusion——"

The Captain would knit his weather-beaten brow and again retire anxiously to his quarters, after begging Gissing to be generous and carry on a while longer. Occasionally, pacing the starboard bridge-deck, sacred to captains, Gissing would glance through the port and see the metaphysical commander bent over sheets of foolscap and thickly wreathed in pipesmoke.

He himself had fallen into a kind of tranced felicity, in which these questions no longer had other than an ingenious interest. His heart was drowned in the engulfing blue. As they made their southing, wind and weather seemed to fall astern, the sun poured with a more golden candour. He stood at the wheel in a tranquil reverie, blithely steering toward some bright belly of cloud that had caught his fancy. Mr. Pointer shook his head when he glanced surreptitiously at the steering recorder, a device that noted graphically every movement of the rudder with a view to promoting economical helmsmanship. Indeed, Gissing's course, as logged on the chart, surprised even himself, so that he forbade the officers taking their noon observations. When Mr. Pointer said something about isobars, the staff-captain replied serenely that he did not expect to find any polar bears in these latitudes.

He had hoped privately for an occasional pirate, and scanned the sea-rim sharply for suspicious topsails. But the ocean, as he remarked, is not crowded. They proceeded, day after day, in a solitary wideness of unblemished colour. The ship, travelling always in the centre of this infinite disk, seemed strangely identified with his own itinerant spirit, watchful at the gist of things, alert at the point which was necessarily, for him, the hub of all existence. He wandered about the *Pomerania's* sagely ordered passages and found her more and more magical. She went on and on, with some strange urgent vitality of her own. Through the fiddleys on the boat deck

N

came a hot oily breath and the steady drumming of her burning heart. From oxter to hawse-hole, from shaft-tunnel to crow's-nest, he explored and loved her. In the whole of her proud, faithful, obedient fabric he divined honour and exultation. Poised upon uncertainty, she was sure. The camber of her white-scrubbed decks, the long, clean sheer of her hull, the concave flare of her bows—what was the amazing joy and rightness of these things? And yet the grotesque passengers regarded her only as a vehicle, to carry them sedatively to some clamouring dock. Fools! She was more lovely than anything they would ever see again! He yearned to drive her endlessly toward that unreachable perimeter of sky.

On land there had been definite horizons, even if disappointing, when reached and examined; but here there was no horizon at all. Every hour it slid and slid over the dark orb of sea. He lost count of time. The tremulous cradling of the *Pomerania*, steadily climbing the long leagues; her noble forecastle solemnly lifting against heaven, then descending with grave beauty into a spread of foaming beryl and snowdrift, seemed one with the rhythm of his pulse and heart.

Perhaps, there had been more than mere ingenuity in his last riddle for the theological skipper. Truly, the subconscious had usurped him. Here he was almost happy, for he was almost unaware of life. It was all blue vacancy and suspension. The sea is the great answer and consoler, for it means either nothing or everything, and so need not tease the brain.

But the passengers, though unobservant, began to murmur ; especially those who had wagered that the *Pomerania* would dock on the eighth day. The world itself, they complained, was created in seven days, and why should so fine a ship take longer to cross a comparatively small ocean ? Urbanely, over coffee and *petits fours,* Gissing argued with them. They were well on their way, he protested; and then, as a hypothetical case, he asked why one destination was more worth visiting than another ? He even quoted Shakespeare on this point—something about " ports and happy havens "—and succeeded in turning the tide of conversation for a while. The mention of Shakespeare suggested to some of the ladies that it would be pleasant, now they all knew each other so well, to put on some amateur theatricals. They compromised by playing charades in the saloon. Another evening Gissing kept them amused by fireworks, which were very lovely against the dark sky. For this purpose he used the emergency rockets, star-shells and coloured flares, much to the distress of Dane, the quartermaster, who had charge of these supplies.

Little by little, however, the querulous protests of the passengers began to weary him. Also, he had been receiving terse memoranda from the Chief Engineer that the coal was getting low in the bunkers and that something must be queer in the navigating department. This seemed very unreasonable. The fixed gaze of Mr. Pointer, perpetually examining the horizon as though he wanted to make sure he would recognise it if they met again, was trying. Even Captain Scottie complained one day that the supply of fresh meat had given out and that the steward had been bringing him tinned beef. Gissing determined upon resolute measures.

He had notice served that on account of possible danger from pirates there would be a general boat drill on the following day—not merely for the crew, but for everyone. He gave a little talk about it in the saloon after dinner, and worked his audience up to quite a pitch of enthusiasm. This would be better than any amateur theatricals, he insisted. Everyone was to act exactly as though in a sudden calamity. They might make up the boat-parties on the basis of congeniality if they wished; five minutes would be given for reaching the stations, without panic or disorder. They should prepare themselves as though they were actually going to leave a sinking ship.

The passengers were delighted with the idea of this novel entertainment. Every soul on board—with the exception of Captain Scottie, who had locked himself in and refused to be disturbed—was properly advertised of the event.

The following day, fortunately, was clear and calm. At noon Gissing blew the syren, fired a rocket from the bridge, and swung the engine telegraph to stop. The ship's orchestra, by his orders, struck up a rollicking air. Quickly and without confusion, amid cries of *Women and children first!* the passengers filed to their allotted places. The crew and officers were all at their stations.

Gissing knocked at Captain Scottie's cabin.

" We are taking to the boats," he said.

" Goad! " cried the skipper. " Wull it be a colleesion? "

" All's clear and the davits are outboard," said Gissing. He had been studying the manual of boat-handling in one of the nautical volumes in the chart-room.

" Auld Hornie! " ejaculated the skipper. " We'll no can salve the specie! Make note of her poseetion, Mr. Gissing! " He hastened to gather his papers, the log, a chronometer, and a large canister of tobacco.

" The Deil's intil't," he said as he hastened to his boat. " I had yon pragmateesm of yours on a lee shore. Two-three hours, I'd have careened ye."

Gissing was ready with his megaphone. From the wing of the bridge he gave the orders.

" Lower away! " and the boats dropped to the passenger rail.

" Avast lowering! " Each boat took in her roster of passengers, who were in high spirits at this unusual excitement.

" Mind your painters! Lower handsomely! "

The boats took the water in orderly fashion, and were cast off. Remaining members of the crew swarmed down the falls. The bandsmen had a boat to themselves, and resumed their tune as soon as they were settled.

Gissing, left alone on the ship, waved for silence.

" Look sharp, man! " cried Captain Scottie. " Honour's satisfied ! Take your place in the boat! "

The passengers applauded, and there was quite a clatter of camera shutter as they snapped the *Pomerania* looming grandly above them.

" Boats are all provisioned and equipped," shouted Gissing. " I've broadcasted your position by radio. The barometer's at Fixed Fair. Pull off now, and 'ware the screw."

He moved the telegraph handle to DEAD SLOW, and the *Pomerania* began to slip forward gently. The boats dropped aft amid a loud miscellaneous outcry. Mr. Pointer was already examining the horizon. Captain Scottie, awakened to the situation, was uttering the language of theology, but not the purport.

" Don't stand up in the boats," megaphoned Gissing. " You're quite all right, there's a ship on the way already. I wirelessed last night."

He slid the telegraph to SLOW, HALF, and then

FULL. Once more the ship creamed through the lifting purple swells. The little flock of boats was soon out of sight.

Alone at the wheel, he realised that a great weight was off his mind. The responsibility of his position had burdened him more than he knew. Now a strange eagerness and joy possessed him. His bubbling wake cut straight and milky across the glittering afternoon. In a ruddy sunset glow, the sea darkened through all tints of violet, amethyst, indigo. The horizon line sharpened so clearly that he could distinguish the tossing profile of waves wetting the sky. " A red sky at night is the sailor's delight," he said to himself. He switched on the port and starboard lights and the masthead lanterns, then lashed the wheel while he went below for supper. He did not know exactly where he was, for he seemed to have steamed clean off the chart; but as he conned the helm that evening, and leaned over the lighted binnacle, he had a feeling that he was not far from some destiny. With cheerful assurance he lashed the wheel again, and turned in. He woke once in the night, and leaped from the hammock with a start. He thought he had heard a sound of barking.

# CHAPTER SIXTEEN

THE next morning he sighted land. Coming out on the bridge, the whole face of things was changed. The sea-colour had lightened to a tawny green; gulls dipped and hovered; away on the horizon lay a soft blue contour. " Land Ho! " he shouted, superbly, and wondered what new country he had discovered. He ran up a hoist of red and yellow signal flags, and steered gaily toward the shore.

It had grown suddenly cold: he had to fetch Captain Scottie's pea-jacket to wear at the wheel. On the long spilling crests, that crumbled and spread running layers of froth in their hurry shoreward, the *Pomerania* rode home. She knew her landfall and seemed to quicken. Steadily swinging on the jade-green surges, she buried her nose almost to the hawse-pipes, then lifted until her streaming forefoot gleamed out of a frilled ruffle of foam.

Gissing, too, was eager. A tingling buoyancy

and impatience took hold of him: he fidgeted with sheer eagerness for life. Land, the beloved stability of our dear and only earth, drew and charmed him. Behind was the senseless, heart-breaking sea. Now he could discern hills rising in a gilded opaline light. In the volatile thin air was a quick sense of strangeness. A new world was close about him: a world that he could see, and feel, and inhale, and yet knew nothing of.

Suddenly a great humility possessed him. He had been forward and silly and vain. He had shouted arrogantly at Beauty, like a noisy tourist in a canyon; and the only answer, after long waiting, had been the paltry diminished echo of his own voice. He thought shamefully of his follies. What matter how you name God or in what words you praise Him? In this new foreign land he would quietly accept things as he found them. The laughter of God was too strange to understand.

No, there was no answer. He was doubly damned, for he had made truth a mere sport of intellectual riddling. The mind, like a spinning flywheel of fatigued steel, was gradually racked to bursting by the conflict of stresses. And yet:

every equilibrium was an opposure of forces. Rotation, if swift enough, creates amazing stability: he had seen how the gyroscope can balance at apparently impossible angles. Perhaps it was so of the mind. If it twirls at high speed it can lean right out over the abyss without collapse. But the stationary mind—he thought of Bishop Borzoi—must keep away from the edge. Try to force it to the edge, it raves in panic. Every mind, very likely, knows its own frailties, and does well to safeguard them. At any rate, that was the most generous interpretation. Most minds, undoubtedly, were uneasy in high places. They doubted their ability to refrain from jumping off. How many bones of fine intellects lay whitening at the foot of the theological cliff——

It seemed to be a lonely coast, and wintry. Patches of snow lay upon the hills, the woods were bare and brown. A bottle-necked harbour opened out before him. He reduced the engines to Dead Slow and glided gaily through the strait. He had been anxious lest his navigation might not be equal to the occasion: he did not want to disgrace himself at this final test. But all seemed to arrange itself with enchanted ease. A steep ledge of ground offered a natural pier, with treestumps for bollards. He let her come gently beyond the spot; reversed the propellers just at the right time, and backed neatly alongside. He moved the telegraph handle to FINISHED WITH ENGINES; ran out the gangplank smartly, and stepped ashore. He moored the vessel fore and aft, and hung out fenders to prevent chafing.

The first thing to do, he said to himself, is to get the lie of the land, and find out whether it is inhabited.

A hillside rising above the water promised a clear view. The stubble grass was dry and frosty; after the warm days at sea the chill was nipping ; but what an elixir of air ! If this is a desert island, he thought, it will be a glorious discovery. His heart was jocund with anticipation. A curious foreign look in the landscape, he thought; quite unlike anything——

Suddenly, where the hill arched against pearly sky, he saw a narrow thread of smoke rising. He halted in alarm. Who might this be, friend or foe? But eager agitation pushed him on. Burning to know, he hurried up to the brow of the hill.

The smoke mounted from a small bonfire of

sticks in a sheltered thicket, where a miraculous
being—who was, as a matter of fact, a rather
ragged and dingy vagabond—was cooking a tin
of stew over the blaze.

Gissing stood, quivering with emotion. Joy
such as he had never known darted through all
the cords of his body. He ran, shouting, in
mirth and terror. In fear, in a passion of love
and knowledge and understanding, he abased
himself and yearned before this marvel. Impossible to have conceived, yet, once seen, utterly
satisfying and the fulfilment of all needs. When
the first transport was over, he laid his head
against this being's knee, he nestled there and
was content. This was the inscrutable, perfect
answer.

"Cripes!" said the puzzled tramp, as he
caressed the nuzzling head. "The purp's loco.
Maybe he's been lost. You might think he'd
never seen a man before."

He was right.

And Gissing sat quietly, his throat resting
upon the soiled knee of a very old and spicy
trouser.

"I have found God," he said.

Presently he thought of the ship. It would

not do to leave her so insecurely moored. Reluctantly, with many a backward glance and a heart full of glory, he left the Presence. He ran to the edge of the hill to look down upon the harbour.

The outlook was puzzlingly altered. He gazed in astonishment. What were those poplars, rising naked into the bright air?—there was something familiar about them. And that little house beyond . . . he stared bewildered.

The great shining breadth of the ocean had shrunk to the roundness of a tiny pond. And the *Pomerania?* He leaned over, shaken with questions. There, beside the bank, was a little plank of wood, a child's plaything, roughly fashioned shipshape: two chips for funnels; red and yellow frosted leaves for flags; a withered dogwood blossom for propeller. He leaned closer, with whirling mind. In the clear, cool surface of the pond he could see the sky mirrored, deeper than any ocean, pellucid, infinite, blue.

He ran up the path to the house. The scuffled, ragged garden lay naked and hard. At the windows, he saw with surprise, were holly wreaths tied with broad red ribbon. On the porch, some battered toys. He opened the door.

A fluttering rosy light filled the room. By the fireplace the puppies—how big they were!—were sitting with Mrs. Spaniel. Joyous uproar greeted him: they flung themselves upon him. Shouts of " Daddy! Daddy! " filled the house, while the young Spaniels stood by more bashfully.

Good Mrs. Spaniel was gratefully moved. Her moist eyes shone brightly in the firelight.

" I knew you'd be home for Christmas, Mr. Gissing," she said. " I've been telling them so all afternoon. Now, children, be still a moment and let me speak. I've been telling you your Daddy would be home in time for a Christmas Eve story. I've got to go and fix that plum pudding."

In her excitement a clear bubble dripped from the tip of her tongue. She caught it in her apron, and hurried to the kitchen.

## CHAPTER SEVENTEEN

THE children insisted on leading him all through the house to show how nicely they had taken care of things. And in every room Gissing saw the marks of riot and wreckage. There were tooth-scars on all furniture-legs; the fringes of rugs were chewed off; there were prints of mud, ink, paints, and what-not, on curtains and wallpapers and coverlets. Poor Mrs. Spaniel kept running anxiously from the kitchen to renew apologies.

"I *did* try to keep 'em in order," she said, "but they seem to bash things when you're not looking."

But Gissing was too happy to stew about such trifles. When the inspection was over, they all sat down by the chimney, and he piled on more logs.

"Well, chilluns," he said, "what do you want Santa Claus to bring you for Christmas?"

" An aunbile! "⎫        ⎧ Groups
" An elephunt! " ⎬ exclaimed ⎨ Bunks
  " A little train ⎭        ⎩ Yelpers
with hammers!"

" A little train with hammers ? " asked
Gissing. " What does he mean ? "

" Oh," said Groups and Bunks, with con-
descending pity, " he means a typewriter. He
calls it a little train because it moves on a track
when you hit it."

A painful apprehension seized him, and he
went hastily to his study. He had not noticed
the typewriter, which Mrs. Spaniel had—too
late—put out of reach. Half the keys were
sticking upright, jammed together and tangled
in a whirl of ribbon; the carriage was strangely
dislocated. And yet even this mischance, which
would once have horrified him, left him unper-
turbed. It's my own fault, he thought : I
shouldn't have left it where they could play
with it. Perhaps God thinks the same when
His creatures make a mess of the dangerous
laws of life.

" A Christmas story ! " the children were
clamouring.

Can it really be Christmas Eve? Gissing

o

thought. Christmas seems to have come very suddenly this year, I haven't really adjusted my mind to it yet.

"All right," he said. "Now sit still and keep quiet. Bunks, give Yelpers a little more room. If there's any bickering Santa Claus might hear it."

He sat in the big chair by the fire, and the three looked upward expectantly from the hearthrug.

"Once upon a time there were three little puppies, who lived in a house in the country in the Canine Estates. And their names were Groups, Bunks, and Yelpers."

The three tails thumped in turn as the names were mentioned, but the children were too excitedly absorbed to interrupt.

"And one year, just before Christmas, they heard a dreadful rumour."

"What's a rumour?" cried Yelpers, alarmed.

This was rather difficult to explain, so Gissing did not attempt it. He began again.

"They heard that Santa Claus might not be able to come because he was so behind with his housework. You see, Santa Claus is a great big Newfoundland dog with a white beard, and he lives in a frosty kennel at the North Pole, all shining with icicles round the roof and windows. But it's so far away from everywhere that poor Santa couldn't get a servant. All the maids who went there refused to stay because it was so cold and lonely, and so far from the movies. Santa Claus was busy in his workshop, making toys; he was busy taking care of the reindeer in their snow-stables; and he didn't have time to wash his dishes. So all summer he just let them pile up and pile up in the kitchen. And when Christmas came near, there was his lovely house in a dreadful state of untidiness. He couldn't go away and leave it like that. And so, if he didn't get his dishes washed and the house cleaned up for Christmas, all the puppies all over the world would have to go without toys. When Groups and Bunks and Yelpers heard this, they were very much worried."

" How did they hear it? " asked Bunks, who was the analytical member of the trio.

" A very sensible question," said Gissing, approvingly. " They heard it from the chipmunk who lives in the wood behind the house. The chipmunk heard it underground."

" In his chipmonastery? " cried Groups. It

was a family joke to call the chipmunk's burrow by that name, and though the puppies did not understand the pun they relished the long word.

" Yes," continued Gissing.  " The reindeer in Santa Claus's stable were so unhappy about the dishes not being washed, and the chance of missing their Christmas frolic, that they broadcasted a radio message.  Their horns are very fine for sending radio; and the chipmunk, sitting at his little wireless outfit, with the receivers over his ears, heard it.  And Chippy told Groups and Bunks and Yelpers.

" So these puppies decided to help Santa Claus.  They didn't know exactly where to find him, but the chipmunk told them the direction, and off they went.  They travelled and travelled, and when they came to the ocean they begged a ride from the seagulls, and each one sat on a seagull's back just as though he was on a little airplane.  They flew and flew, and at last they came to Santa Claus's house.  Through the stable-walls, which were made of ice they could see the reindeer stamping in their stalls.  In the big workshop, where Santa Claus was busy making toys, they could hear a lively sound of hammering.  The big red sleigh was standing outside the stables, all ready to be hitched up to the reindeer.

"They slipped into Santa Claus's house quickly and quietly, so no one would see or hear them. The house was in a terrible state, but they set to work to clean up. Groups found the vacuum cleaner and sucked up all the crumbs from the dining-room rug. Bunks ran upstairs and made Santa Claus's bed for him and swept the floors and put clean towels in the bathroom. And Yelpers hurried into the kitchen and washed the dishes, and scrubbed the pots, and polished the egg-stains off the silver spoons, and emptied the ice-box pan. All working hard, they got through very soon, and made Santa Claus's house as clean as any house could be. They fixed the window-shades so that they would all hang level, not just anyhow, as poor Santa had them. Then, when everything was spick and span, they ran outdoors again and beckoned the seagulls. They climbed on the gulls' backs, and away they flew homeward."

"Was Santa Claus pleased?" asked Bunks.

"Indeed he was, when he came back from his workshop, very tired after making toys all day——"

"What kind of toys did he make? exclaimed Yelpers anxiously. "Did he make a typewriter?"

"He made every kind of toy. And when he saw how his house had been cleaned up, he thought the fairies must have done it. He lit his pipe, and filled a thermos bottle with hot cocoa to keep him warm on his long journey. Then he put on his red coat, and his long boots, and his fur cap, and went out to harness the reindeer. That very night he drove off with his sleigh packed full of toys for all the puppies in the world. In fact, he was so pleased that he loaded his big bag with more toys than he had ever carried before. And that was how a queer thing happened."

They waited in eager suspense.

"You know, Santa Claus always drives into the Canine Estates by the little back road through the woods, where the chipmunk lives. You know the gateway, at the bend in the lane: well, it's rather narrow, and Santa Claus's sleigh is very wide. And this time, because his bag had so many toys in it, the bag bulged over the edge of the sleigh, and one corner of the bag caught on the gatepost as he drove by.

Three toys fell out, and what do you suppose they were? "

" An aunbile! "

" An elphunt! "

" A typewriter! "

" Yes, that's quite right. And it happened that the chipmunk was out that night, digging up some nuts for his Christmas dinner, a little sad because he had no presents to give his children; and he found the three toys. He took them home to the little chipmunks, and they were tremendously pleased. That was only fair, because if it hadn't been for the chipmunk and his radio set, *no one* would have had any toys that Christmas."

" Did Santa Claus have any more typewriters in his bag? " asked Yelpers gravely.

" Oh, yes, he had plenty more of everything. And when he got to the house where Groups and Bunks and Yelpers lived, he slid down the chimney and took a look round. He didn't see any crumbs on the floor, or any toys lying about not put away, so he filled the stockings with all kinds of lovely things, and an aunbile and an elphunt and a typewriter."

" What did the puppies say? " they inquired.

" They were sound asleep upstairs, and didn't know anything about it until Christmas morning. Come on now, it's time for bed."

" We can undress ourselves now," said Groups.

" Will you tuck me in? " said Bunks.

" You're sure he had another typewriter in his bag? " said Yelpers.

They scrambled upstairs.

Later, when the house was quiet, Gissing went out to the kitchen to see Mrs. Spaniel. She was diligently rolling pastry, and her nose was white with flour.

" Oh, sir, I'm glad you got home in time for Christmas," she said. " The children were counting on it. Did you have a successful trip, sir? "

" Every trip is successful when you get home again," said Gissing. " I suppose the shops will be open late to-night, won't they? I'm going to run down to the village to get some toys."

Before leaving the house, he went down to the cellar to see if the furnace was all right. He was amazed to see how naturally and cheerfully he had slipped back into the old sense of responsibility. Where was the illusory freedom he had dreamed of? Even the epiphany on the hilltop now seemed a distant miracle. That fearful happiness might never come again. And yet here, among the familiar, difficult minutiæ of home, what a lightness he felt. A great phrase from the prayer-book came to his mind— " Whose service is perfect freedom."

Ah, he said to himself, it is all very well to wear a crown of thorns, and indeed every sensitive creature carries one in secret. But there are times when it ought to be worn cocked over one ear.

He opened the furnace door. A bright glow filled the fire-box: he could hear a stir and singing in the boiler, and the rustle of warm pipes chuckled quietly through winter nights of storm. Over the coals hovered a magic, evasive flicker, the very soul of fire. It was a pentecostal flame, perfect and heavenly in tint, the essence of pure colour, a clear immortal blue.

**THE END**

# A LIST OF VOLUMES ISSUED IN
# THE TRAVELLERS' LIBRARY

3s. 6d. net each

JONATHAN CAPE LTD.
THIRTY BEDFORD SQUARE
LONDON

WILLIAM HEINEMANN LTD.
NINETY-NINE GT. RUSSELL ST.
LONDON

# THE TRAVELLERS' LIBRARY

✳

A series of books in all branches of literature designed for the pocket, or for the small house where shelf space is scarce. Though the volumes measure only 7 inches by 4¾ inches, the page is arranged so that the margins are not unreasonably curtailed nor legibility sacrificed. The books are of a uniform thickness irrespective of the number of pages, and the paper, specially manufactured for the series, is remarkably opaque, even when it is thinnest.

A semi-flexible form of binding has been adopted, as a safeguard against the damage inevitably associated with hasty packing. The cloth is of a particularly attractive shade of blue and has the author's name stamped in gold on the back. Each volume costs 3s. 6d. net (postage 3d.).

✳

1. CAN SUCH THINGS BE ?    A volume of Stories
   by Ambrose Bierce

❡ ' Bierce never wastes a word, never coins a too startling phrase ; he secures his final effect, a cold thrill of fear, by a simple, yet subtle, realism.    No anthology of short stories, limited to a score or so, would be complete without an example of his unique artistry.' *Morning Post*

2. THE BLACK DOG.    A volume of Stories
   by A. E. Coppard

❡ ' Mr. Coppard is a born story-teller.    The book is filled with a variety of delightful stuff : no one who is interested in good writing in general, and good short stories in particular, should miss it.' *Spectator*

3. THE AUTOBIOGRAPHY of a SUPER-TRAMP
   by W. H. Davies. With a preface by G. Bernard Shaw

❡ Printed as it was written, it is worth reading for its literary style alone.    The author tells us with inimitable quiet modesty of how he begged and stole his way across America and through England and Wales until his travelling days were cut short by losing his right foot while attempting to ' jump ' a train.

## 4. BABBITT   A Novel
### by Sinclair Lewis

¶ 'One of the greatest novels I have read for a long time.
*H. G. Wells*          'Babbitt is a triumph.'   *Hugh Walpole*
'His work has that something extra, over and above, which
makes the work of art, and it is signed in every line with the
unique personality of the author.'   *Rebecca West*


## 5. THE CRAFT OF FICTION
### by Percy Lubbock

¶ 'No more substantial or more charming volume of criticism
has been published in our time.'   *Observer*
'To say that this is the best book on the subject is probably true;
but it is more to the point to say that it is the only one.'
*Times Literary Supplement*


## 6. EARLHAM
### by Percy Lubbock

¶ 'The book seems too intimate to be reviewed.   We want to be
allowed to read it, and to dream over it, and keep silence about
it.   His judgment is perfect, his humour is true and ready; his
touch light and prim; his prose is exact and clean and full
of music.'   *Times*


## 7. WIDE SEAS & MANY LANDS A Personal Narrative
### by Arthur Mason.
### With an Introduction by MAURICE BARING

¶ 'This is an extremely entertaining, and at the same time, moving
book.   We are in the presence of a born writer.   We read with
the same mixture of amazement and delight that fills us through-
out a Conrad novel.'   *New Statesman*


## 8. SELECTED PREJUDICES   A book of Essays
### by H. L. Mencken

¶ 'He is exactly the kind of man we are needing, an iconoclast,
a scoffer at ideals, a critic with whips and scorpions who does
not hesitate to deal with literary, social and political humbugs
in the one slashing fashion.'   *English Review*

## 9. THE MIND IN THE MAKING  An Essay
### by James Harvey Robinson

¶ ' For me, I think James Harvey Robinson is going to be almost as important as was Huxley in my adolescence, and William James in later years. It is a cardinal book. I question whether in the long run people may not come to it, as making a new initiative into the world's thought and methods.' *From the Introduction by* H. G. WELLS

## 10. THE WAY OF ALL FLESH  A Novel
### by Samuel Butler

¶ 'It drives one almost to despair of English Literature when one sees so extraordinary a study of English life as Butler's posthumous *Way of All Flesh* making so little impression. Really, the English do not deserve to have great men.' *George Bernard Shaw*

## 11. EREWHON  A Satire
### by Samuel Butler

¶ 'To lash the age, to ridicule vain pretension, to expose hypocrisy, to deride humbug in education, politics and religion, are tasks beyond most men's powers; but occasionally, very occasionally, a bit of genuine satire secures for itself more than a passing nod of recognition. *Erewhon* is such a satire. . . . The best of its kind since *Gulliver's Travels*.' *Augustine Birrell*

## 12. EREWHON REVISITED  A Satire
### by Samuel Butler

¶ ' He waged a sleepless war with the mental torpor of the prosperous, complacent England around him; a Swift with the soul of music in him, and completely sane; a liberator of humanity operating with the wit and malice and coolness of Mephistopheles.' *Manchester Guardian*

## 13. ADAM AND EVE AND PINCH ME  Stories
### by A. E. Coppard

¶ Mr. Coppard's implicit theme is the closeness of the spiritual world to the material; the strange, communicative sympathy which strikes through two temperaments and suddenly makes them one. He deals with those sudden impulses under which secrecy is broken down for a moment, and personality revealed as under a flash of spiritual lightning.

### 14. DUBLINERS   A volume of Stories
#### by James Joyce

¶ A collection of fifteen short stories by the author of *Ulysses*. They are all of them brave, relentless, and sympathetic pictures of Dublin life ; realistic, perhaps, but not crude ; analytical, but not repugnant.   No modern writer has greater significance than Mr. Joyce, whose conception and practice of the short story is certainly unique and certainly vital.

### 15. DOG AND DUCK
#### by Arthur Machen

¶ ' As a literary artist, Mr. Arthur Machen has few living equals, and that is very far indeed from being his only, or even his greatest, claim on the suffrages of English readers.'   *Sunday Times*

### 16. KAI LUNG'S GOLDEN HOURS
#### by Ernest Bramah

¶ ' It is worthy of its forerunner.   There is the same plan, exactitude, working-out and achievement ; and therefore complete satisfaction in the reading.'   *From the Preface by* HILAIRE BELLOC

### 17. ANGELS & MINISTERS, AND OTHER PLAYS
#### by Laurence Housman
Imaginary portraits of political characters done in dialogue— Queen Victoria, Disraeli, Gladstone, Parnell, Joseph Chamberlain, and Woodrow Wilson.

¶ ' It is all so good that one is tempted to congratulate Mr. Housman on a true masterpiece.'   *Times*

### 18. THE WALLET OF KAI LUNG
#### by Ernest Bramah

¶ ' Something worth doing and done. . . .   It was a thing intended, wrought out, completed and established.   Therefore it was destined to endure, and, what is more important, it was a success.'   *Hilaire Belloc*

\*

## 19. TWILIGHT IN ITALY
### by D. H. Lawrence

¶ This volume of travel vignettes in North Italy was first published in 1916. Since then Mr. Lawrence has increased the number of his admirers year by year. In *Twilight in Italy* they will find all the freshness and vigour of outlook which they have come to expect from its author.

## 20. THE DREAM   A Novel
### by H. G. Wells

¶ 'It is the richest, most generous and absorbing thing that Mr. Wells has given us for years and years.' *Daily News*
'I find this book as close to being magnificent as any book that I have ever read. It is full of inspiration and life.'
*Daily Graphic*

## 21. ROMAN PICTURES
### by Percy Lubbock

¶ Pictures of life as it is lived—or has been or might be lived—among the pilgrims and colonists in Rome of more or less English speech.
'A book of whimsical originality and exquisite workmanship, and worthy of one of the best prose writers of our time.'
*Sunday Times*

## 22. CLORINDA WALKS IN HEAVEN
### by A. E. Coppard

¶ 'Genius is a hard-ridden word, and has been put by critics at many puny ditches, but Mr. Coppard sets up a fence worthy of its mettle. He shows that in hands like his the English language is as alive as ever, and that there are still infinite possibilities in the short story.' *Outlook*

## 23. MARIUS THE EPICUREAN
### by Walter Pater

¶ Walter Pater was at the same time a scholar of wide sympathies and a master of the English language. In this, his best known work, he describes with rare delicacy of feeling and insight the religious and philosophic tendencies of the Roman Empire at the time of Antoninus Pius as they affected the mind and life of the story's hero.

## 24. THE WHITE SHIP   Stories
### by Aino Kallas
With an Introduction by JOHN GALSWORTHY

¶ 'The writer has an extraordinary sense of atmosphere.'
*Times Literary Supplement*
'Stories told convincingly and well, with a keen perceptive for
natural beauty.'  *Nation*

## 25. MULTITUDE AND SOLITUDE   A Novel
### by John Masefield

¶ 'As well conceived and done, as rich in observation of the
world, as profound where it needs to be profound, as any novel
of recent writing.'  *Outlook*
'This is no common book.  It is a book which not merely
touches vital things.  It is vital.'  *Daily News*

## 26. SPRING SOWING   Stories
### by Liam O'Flaherty

¶ 'Nothing seems to escape Mr. O'Flaherty's eye; his brain
turns all things to drama; and his vocabulary is like a river in
spate.  *Spring Sowing* is a book to buy, or to borrow, or, yes,
to steal.'  *Bookman*

## 27. WILLIAM   A Novel
### by E. H. Young

¶ 'An extraordinary good book, penetrating and beautiful.'
*Allan Monkhouse*
'All its characters are very real and alive, and William himself
is a masterpiece.'  *May Sinclair*

## 28. THE COUNTRY OF THE POINTED FIRS
### by Sarah Orne Jewett

¶ 'The young student of American literature in the far distant
future will take up this book and say " a masterpiece ! " as
proudly as if he had made it.  It will be a message in a universal
language—the one message that even the scythe of Time spares.'
*From the Preface by* WILLA CATHER

## 29. GRECIAN ITALY
### by Henry James Forman

¶ 'It has been said that if you were shown Taormina in a vision you would not believe it. If the reader has been in Grecian Italy before he reads this book, the magic of its pages will revive old memories and induce a severe attack of nostalgia.' *From the Preface by* H. FESTING JONES

## 30. WUTHERING HEIGHTS
### by Emily Brontë

¶ 'It is a very great book. You may read this grim story of lost and thwarted human creatures on a moor at any age and come under its sway.' *From the Introduction by* ROSE MACAULAY

## 31. ON A CHINESE SCREEN
### by W. Somerset Maugham

¶ A collection of sketches of life in China. Mr. Somerset Maugham writes with equal certainty and vigour whether his characters are Chinese or European. There is a tenderness and humour about the whole book which makes the reader turn eagerly to the next page for more.

## 32. A FARMER'S LIFE
¶ ### by George Bourne

The life story of a tenant-farmer of fifty years ago in which the author of *The Bettesworth Book* and *The Memoirs of a Surrey Labourer* draws on his memory for a picture of the every-day life of his immediate forebears, the Smiths, farmers and handicraft men, who lived and died on the border of Surrey and Hampshire.

## 33. TWO PLAYS. *The Cherry Orchard & The Sea Gull*
### by Anton Tchekoff. Translated by George Calderon

¶ Tchekoff had that fine comedic spirit which relishes the incongruity between the actual disorder of the world with the underlying order. He habitually mingled tragedy (which is life seen close at hand) with comedy (which is life seen at a distance). His plays are tragedies with the texture of comedy.

## 34. THE MONK AND THE HANGMAN'S DAUGHTER
### by Ambrose Bierce

¶ 'They are stories which the discerning are certain to welcome. They are evidence of very unusual powers, and when once they have been read the reader will feel himself impelled to dig out more from the same pen.' *Westminster Gazette*

## 35. CAPTAIN MARGARET   A Novel
### by John Masefield

¶ 'His style is crisp, curt and vigorous.   He has the Stevensonian sea-swagger, the Stevensonian sense of beauty and poetic spirit. Mr. Masefield's descriptions ring true and his characters carry conviction.'   *The Observer*

## 36. BLUE WATER
### by Arthur Sturges Hildebrand

¶ This book gives the real feeling of life on a small cruising yacht ; the nights on deck with the sails against the sky, long fights with head winds by mountainous coasts to safety in forlorn little island ports, and constant adventure free from care.

## 37. STORIES FROM DE MAUPASSANT
### Translated by Elizabeth Martindale

¶ 'His "story" engrosses the non-critical, it holds the critical too at the first reading. . . .   That is the real test of art, and it is because of the inobtrusiveness of this workmanship, that for once the critic and the reader may join hands without awaiting the verdict of posterity.' *From the Introduction by* FORD MADOX FORD

## 38. WHILE THE BILLY BOILS   First Series
### by Henry Lawson

¶ These stories are written by the O. Henry of Australia.   They tell of men and dogs, of cities and plains, of gullies and ridges, of sorrow and happiness, and of the fundamental goodness that is hidden in the most unpromising of human soil.

## 46. WHEN THE BOUGH BREAKS
### by Naomi Mitchison

Stories of the time when Rome was crumbling to ruin

¶ 'Interesting, delightful, and fresh as morning dew. The connoisseur in short stories will turn to some pages in this volume again and again with renewed relish.' *Times Literary Supplement*

## 47. THE FLYING BO'SUN
### by Arthur Mason

¶ 'What makes the book remarkable is the imaginative power which has recreated these events so vividly that even the supernatural ones come with the shock and the conviction with which actual supernatural events might come.' *From the Introduction by* EDWIN MUIR

## 48. LATER DAYS
### by W. H. Davies

A pendant to *The Autobiography of a Super-Tramp*

¶ 'The self-portrait is given with disarming, mysterious, and baffling directness, and the writing has the same disarmingness and simpleness.' *Observer*

## 49. THE EYES OF THE PANTHER Stories
### by Ambrose Bierce

¶ It is said that these tales were originally rejected by virtually every publisher in the country. Bierce was a strange man ; in 1914 at the age of seventy-one he set out for Mexico and has never been heard of since. His stories are as strange as his life, but this volume shows him as a master of his art.

## 50. IN DEFENCE OF WOMEN
### by H. L. Mencken

¶ 'All I design by the book is to set down in more or less plain form certain ideas that practically every civilized man and woman holds *in petto*, but that have been concealed hitherto by the vast mass of sentimentalities swathing the whole woman question.' *From the Author's Introduction*

### 51. VIENNESE MEDLEY   A Novel
####   by Edith O'Shaughnessy

❡ ' It is told with infinite tenderness, with many touches of grave or poignant humour, in a very beautiful book, which no lover of fiction should allow to pass unread.   A book which sets its writer definitely in the first rank of living English novelists.' *Sunday Times*

### 52. PRECIOUS BANE   A Novel
####   by Mary Webb

❡ ' She has a style of exquisite beauty ; which yet has both force and restraint, simplicity and subtlety ; she has fancy and wit, delicious humour and pathos.   She sees and knows men aright as no other novelist does.   She has, in short, genius.'   *Mr. Edwin Pugh*

### 53. THE INFAMOUS JOHN FRIEND
####   by Mrs. R. S. Garnett

❡ This book, though in form an historical novel, claims to rank as a psychological study.   It is an attempt to depict a character which, though destitute of the common virtues of every-day life, is gifted with qualities that compel love and admiration.

### 54. HORSES AND MEN
####   by Sherwood Anderson

❡ '*Horses and Men* confirms our indebtedness to the publishers who are introducing his work here.   It has a unity beyond that of its constant Middle-west setting.   A man of poetic vision, with an intimate knowledge of particular conditions of life, here looks out upon a world that seems singularly material only because he unflinchingly accepts its actualities.'   *Morning Post*

### 55. SELECTED ESSAYS
####   by Samuel Butler

❡ This volume contains the following essays :

| | |
|---|---|
| The Humour of Homer | How to Make the Best of Life |
| Quis Desiderio . . .? | The Sanctuary of Montrigone |
| Ramblings in Cheapside | A Medieval Girl's School |
| The Aunt, the Nieces, and the Dog | Art in the Valley of Saas |
| | Thought and Language |

## 56. A POET'S PILGRIMAGE
### by W. H. Davies

¶ *A Poet's Pilgrimage* recounts the author's impressions of his native Wales on his return after many years' absence. The author tells of a walking tour he went through Wales. He stayed in cheap rooms and ate in the small wayside inns. The result is a vivid picture of the Welsh people, the towns and countryside.

## 57. GLIMPSES OF UNFAMILIAR JAPAN. First Series
### by Lafcadio Hearn

¶ Nearly all the books which have been written about Japan have either been compiled from official records, or have been superficial sketches of a passing traveller. Of the inner life of the Japanese we know practically nothing, their religion, superstitions, ways of thought. In this book Lafcadio Hearn reveals something of the people and their customs as they are.

## 58. GLIMPSES OF UNFAMILIAR JAPAN. Second Series
### by Lafcadio Hearn

¶ These are sketches by an acute observer and a master of English prose, of a Nation in transition—of the lingering remains of Old Japan, to-day only a memory, of its gardens, its beliefs, customs, gods and devils, of its wonderful kindliness and charm—and of the New Japan, struggling against odds towards new ideals.

## 59. THE TRAVELS OF MARCO POLO
### Edited by Manuel Komroff

¶ When Marco Polo arrived at the court of the Great Khan, Pekin had just been rebuilt and made the capital of China. Kublai Khan was at the height of his glory. Marco Polo rose rapidly in favour and became governor of an important district. In this way he gained first-hand knowledge of a great civilization and described it in his travels with astounding accuracy and detail.

## 60. SELECTED PREJUDICES. Second Series
### by H. L. Mencken

¶ 'What a master of the straight left in appreciation! Everybody who wishes to see how common sense about books and authors can be made exhilarating should acquire this delightful book.'

*Morning Post*

## 61. THE WORLD'S BACK DOORS
### by Max Murray
With an introduction by HECTOR BOLITHO

¶ This book has been never before published. It is not an account so much of places as of people. The journey round the world was begun with about enough money to buy one meal, and continued for 66,000 miles. There are periods as a longshore man and as a sailor, and a Chinese guard and a night watchman, and as a hobo.

## 62. THE EVOLUTION OF AN INTELLECTUAL
### by J. Middleton Murry

¶ These essays were written during and immediately after the Great War and published in 1920. The author says that they record the painful stages by which he passed from the so-called intellectual state to the state of being what he now considers to be a reasonable man.

## 63. THE RENAISSANCE
### by Walter Pater

¶ This English classic contains studies of those 'supreme artists,' Michelangelo and Da Vinci, and of Botticelli, Della Robia, Mirandola, and others, who ' have a distinct faculty of their own by which they convey to us a peculiar quality of pleasure which we cannot get elsewhere.' There is no romance or subtlety in the work of these masters too fine for Pater to distinguish in superb English.

## 64. THE ADVENTURES OF A WANDERER
### by Sydney Walter Powell

¶ The author has described the story of his roving years. Throwing up a position in the Civil Service in Natal because he preferred movement and freedom to monotony and security, he started his wanderings by enlisting in an Indian Ambulance Corps in the South African War. Afterwards he wandered all over the world.

## 65. 'RACUNDRA'S' FIRST CRUISE
### by Arthur Ransome

¶ This is the story of the building of an ideal yacht which would be a cruising boat that one man could manage if need be, but on which three people could live comfortably. The adventures of the cruise are skilfully and vividly told.

## 66. THE MARTYRDOM OF MAN
### by Winwood Reade

¶ 'Few sketches of universal history by one single author have been written. One book that has influenced me very strongly is *The Martyrdom of Man*. This " dates," as people say, nowadays, and it has a fine gloom of its own ; but it is still an extraordinarily inspiring presentation of human history as one consistent process.' *H. G. Wells* in *The Outline of History*.

## 67. THE AUTOBIOGRAPHY OF MARK RUTHERFORD With an introduction by H. W. Massingham

¶ Because of its honesty, delicacy and simplicity of portraiture, this book has always had a curious grip upon the affections of its readers. Every student must feel ' Ah, I have passed that way, have thought thus.' An English Amiel, inheriting to his comfort an English Old Crome landscape, he freed and strengthened his own spirit as he will his reader's.

## 68. THE DELIVERANCE
### by Mark Rutherford

¶ Once read, Hale White [Mark Rutherford] is never forgotten. But he is not yet approached through the highways of English letters. To the lover of his work, nothing can be more attractive than the truth and delicacy of his art, and the pure and serene atmosphere of thought in which it moves.

## 69. THE REVOLUTION IN TANNER'S LANE
### by Mark Rutherford

¶ ' Since Bunyan, English Puritanism has produced one imaginative genius of the highest order. To my mind, our fiction contains no more perfectly drawn pictures of English life in its recurring emotional contrast of excitement and repose more valuable to the historian, or more stimulating to the imaginative reader.' *H. W. Massingham*

## 70. ASPECTS OF SCIENCE. First Series
### by J. W. N. Sullivan

¶ The papers which make up this volume have been selected because, although they deal with different aspects of various scientific ideas, yet they do illustrate, more or less, one point of view. This book tries to show one or two of the many reasons why science may be interesting for people who are not specialists as well as for those who are.


## 71. MASTRO-DON GESUALDO
### Giovanni Verga.   Translated by D. H. Lawrence

¶ Verga, who died in 1922, is recognized in Italy as the greatest of Italian writers of fiction except Manzoni. He can claim a place beside Hardy and the Russians. ' It is a fine, full tale, a fine full picture of life, with a bold beauty of its own which Mr. Lawrence must have relished greatly as he translated it.'
*Observer*


## 72. THE MISSES MALLETT
### by E. H. Young

¶ The virtue of this quiet and accomplished piece of writing lies in its quality and in its character-drawing; to summarize it would be to give no idea of its charm. Neither realism nor romance, it is a book by a writer of insight and sensibility.


## 73. SELECTED ESSAYS. First Series
### by Sir Edmund Gosse, C.B.

¶ ' The prose of Sir Edmund Gosse makes no concession to the passing of years. It is as rich in the colour of young imagination as in the mellow harmony of judgment. No living critic has so sympathetically revealed the art in the artist, and the artist in his art. For his rare and invaluable gift Sir Edmund Gosse's literary kit-kats will continue to be read with avidity long after the greater part of the academic criticism of the century is swept away upon the lumber-heap.' *Daily Telegraph*

## 74. WHERE THE BLUE BEGINS
### by Christopher Morley

¶ A delicious satirical fantasy, in which humanity wears a dog-collar.

'Mr. Morley is a master of consequent inconsequence. His humour and irony are excellent, and his satire is only the more salient for the delicate and ingenuous fantasy in which it is set.'
*Manchester Guardian*

## 75. JAVA HEAD
### by Joseph Hergesheimer

¶ Mr. Hergesheimer has explored the European literary tradition and made of it something distinctively American. In his art he has created a connoisseur's world of his own ; a world of colourful bric-à-brac—of ships and rustling silks and old New England houses—a world in which the rarest and most perplexing of emotions are caught and expressed for the perceptible moment as in austerely delicate porcelain. *Java Head* is a novel of grave and lasting beauty.

## 76. CONFESSIONS OF A YOUNG MAN
### by George Moore

¶ 'Mr. Moore, true to his period and to his genius, stripped himself of everything that might stand between him and the achievement of his artistic object. He does not ask you to admire this George Moore. He merely asks you to observe him beyond good and evil as a constant plucked from the bewildering flow of eternity.' *Humbert Wolfe*

## 77. THE BAZAAR. Stories
### by Martin Armstrong

¶ 'These stories have considerable range of subject, but in general they are stay-at-home tales, depicting cloistered lives and delicate finely fibred minds. . . . Mr. Armstrong writes beautifully.' *Nation and Athenæum*

## 78. SIDE SHOWS. Essays
### by J. B. Atkins
### With an Introduction by JAMES BONE

¶ Mr. J. B. Atkins, war correspondent in four wars, the London editor of a great English paper, then Paris correspondent of another, and latterly the editor of the *Spectator*, has long been known by his colleagues as one of the most informed and refreshing of writers. *Side Shows*, which was published in 1908, contained many inimitable sketches and fancies that had appeared in the press. His subjects are briefly London and the sea.

## 79. SHORT TALKS WITH THE DEAD
### by Hilaire Belloc

¶ In this series of twenty-nine essays Mr. Hilaire Belloc succeeds in attaining his usual high level of pungent and witty writing. The subjects vary widely and include an imaginary talk with the spirits of Charles I, the barber of Louis XIV, Napoleon, bad verse, Venice, fakes, eclipses, Byron and the famous dissertation on the Nordic Man.

## 80. ORIENT EXPRESS
### by John dos Passos

¶ The fact that the tracks led East is accidental; the real thing is that tracks lead. The chief thing that will make this book of interest to people is that, as well as being the temperature chart of an unfortunate sufferer from the travelling disease, it deals with places shaken by the heavy footsteps of History, manifesting itself as usual by plague, famine, murder, sudden death and depreciated currency. But underneath the book is an ode to railroad travel.

## 81. SELECTED ESSAYS. Second Series
### by Sir Edmund Gosse, C.B.

¶ A second volume of essays personally chosen by Sir Edmund Gosse from the wide field of his literary work. One is delighted with the width of his appreciation which enables him to write with equal charm on *Wycherley* and on *How to Read the Bible*.

## 82. ON THE EVE
#### by Ivan Turgenev. Translated by Constance Garnett

¶ To the large humanity of Turgenev criticism may yield. His is the art which intensifies and enlarges men's sympathies on a universal scale. In his characters is something of the width and depth which so astounds us in the creations of Shakespeare. *On the Eve* is a quiet work, yet over which the growing consciousness of coming events casts its heavy shadow. Turgenev, even as he sketched the ripening love of a young girl, has made us feel the dawning aspirations of a nation.

## 83. FATHERS AND CHILDREN
#### by Ivan Turgenev. Translated by Constance Garnett

¶ ' As a piece of art *Fathers and Children* is the most powerful of all Turgenev's works. The figure of Bazarov is not only the political centre of the book, against which the other characters show up in their respective significance, but a figure in which the eternal tragedy of man's impotence and insignificance is realized in scenes of a most ironical human drama.' *Edward Garnett*

## 84. SMOKE
#### by Ivan Turgenev. Translated by Constance Garnett

¶ In this novel Turgenev sees and reflects, even in the shifting phases of political life, that which is universal in human nature. We are shown the permanent attitude behind its changing expression in thought and in action ; in the pictured individual we see the recurrent type. His work is compassionate, beautiful, unique ; in the sight of his fellow-craftsmen always marvellous and often perfect.

## 85. PORGY. A Tale
#### by du Bose Heyward

¶ This fascinating book gives a vivid and intimate insight into the lives of a group of American negroes, from whom Porgy stands out, rich in humour and tragedy. The author's description of a hurricane is reminiscent in its power.

## 86. FRANCE AND THE FRENCH
### by Sisley Huddleston

¶ 'There has been nothing of its kind published since the War. His book is a repository of facts marshalled with judgment; as such it should assist in clearing away a whole maze of misconceptions and prejudices, and serve as a sort of pocket encyclopædia of modern France.' *Times Literary Supplement*

## 88. CLOUD CUCKOO LAND. A Novel of Sparta
### by Naomi Mitchison

¶ 'It is nothing short of genius that Mrs. Mitchison displays in her romance. She seems indeed by imaginative insight to have got into Greece.' *Sunday Times*
'Rich and frank in passions, and rich, too, in the detail which helps to make feigned life seem real.' *Times Literary Supplement*

## 89. A PRIVATE IN THE GUARDS
### by Stephen Graham

¶ In his own experiences as a soldier Stephen Graham has conserved the half-forgotten emotions of a nation in arms. Here in all its tragedy is mindless courage, faith born of a great emotion. Above all he makes us feel the stark brutality and horror of actual war, the valour which is more than valour, and the disciplined endurance which is human and therefore the more terrifying.

## 90. THUNDER ON THE LEFT
### by Christopher Morley

¶ 'It is personal to every reader, it will become for every one a reflection of himself. I fancy that here, as always where work is fine and true, the author has created something not as he would but as he must, and is here an interpreter of a world more wonderful than he himself knows.' *Hugh Walpole*

## 91. THE MOON AND SIXPENCE
### by Somerset Maugham

¶ A remarkable picture of a genius.

' Mr. Maugham has given us a ruthless and penetrating study in personality with a savage truthfulness of delineation and an icy contempt for the heroic and the sentimental.' *The Times*

## 92. THE CASUARINA TREE
### by W. Somerset Maugham

¶ A set of six intensely dramatic stories in which the stain of the East falls deeply on the lives of English men and women. Mr. Maugham remains cruelly aloof from his characters. On passion and its culminating tragedy he looks with unmoved detachment, ringing the changes without comment and yet with little cynicism. These tales are brilliant and hard.

## 93. A POOR MAN'S HOUSE
### by Stephen Reynolds

¶ Vivid and intimate pictures of a Devonshire fisherman's life, on sea and land.

' Compact, harmonious, without a single—I won't say false—but uncertain note, true in aim, sentiment and expression, precise and imaginative, never precious, but containing here and there an absolutely priceless phrase. . . .' *Joseph Conrad*

## 94. WILLIAM BLAKE
### by Arthur Symons

¶ When Blake spoke the first word of the nineteenth century there was none to hear it ; and now that his message has penetrated the world, and is slowly remaking it, few are conscious of the man who first voiced it. This lack of knowledge is remedied in Mr. Symons' work.

## 95. A LITERARY PILGRIM IN ENGLAND
### by Edward Thomas

¶ A book about the homes and resorts of English writers, from John Aubrey, Cowper, Gilbert White, Cobbett, Wordsworth, Burns, Borrow and Lamb, to Swinburne, Stephenson, Meredith, W. H. Hudson and H. Belloc. Each chapter is a miniature biography and at the same time a picture of the man and his work and environment.

## 96. NAPOLEON : THE LAST PHASE
### by The Earl of Rosebery

¶ The idolatry and hatred which Napoleon inspired survived him too long to allow the play of reason. Even now it is not easy to gaze dispassionately at this dazzling luminary. Of books and memoirs about Napoleon there is indeed no end, but of the veracious books such as this book by Lord Rosebery there are remarkably few. This book does not deal with the speculation, it aims to penetrate the deliberate darkness which surrounds the last act of the Napoleonic drama.

## 97. THE POCKET BOOK OF POEMS AND SONGS FOR THE OPEN AIR
### Compiled by Edward Thomas

¶ This anthology is meant to please those lovers of poetry and the country who like a book that can always lighten some of their burdens or give wings to their delight, whether in the open air by day, or under the roof at evening; in it is gathered much of the finest English poetry, and that poetry, at its best can hardly avoid the open air. It is a book that will endure the sunshine and the firelight and give out an equal sweetness on the table and on the sward.

## 98. SAFETY PINS : ESSAYS
### by Christopher Morley
### With an Introduction by H. M. TOMLINSON

¶ Very many readers will be glad of the opportunity to meet Mr. Morley in the rôle of the gentle essayist. He is an author who is content to move among his fellows, to note, to reflect, and to write genially and urbanely; to love words for their sound as well as for their value in expression of thought

## 99. THE BLACK SOUL : A Novel
### by Liam O'Flaherty

¶ The Black Soul of the story is a man shattered mentally and physically by war and despairing of life. Nature brings him back step by step to health and vigour. It is the fight of Nature against the evil of civilization

'*The Black Soul* overwhelms one like a storm. . . . Nothing like it has been written by any Irish writer.' Æ in *The Irish Statesman*

100. CHRISTINA ALBERTA'S FATHER :
   Novel
   by H. G. Wells

¶ ' The best living writer of imaginative fiction in England. . . .
As first reading the book is utterly beyond criticism ; all the
   characters are delightfully genuine.' *Spectator*
' Brimming over with Wellsian insight, humour and invention.
No one but Mr. Wells could have written the whole book and
   given it such verve and sparkle.' *Westminster Gazette*

★

Beginning with 1928 *The Travellers' Library* will be published as a joint enterprise by Jonathan Cape Ltd. and William
Heinemann Ltd. The new volumes announced to appear
during the spring of 1928 include also those to be published
by both firms. The series as a whole or any title in the
series can be ordered from either William Heinemann or
Jonathan Cape. Booksellers' only care must be not to dupli-
cate their orders.

Made and Printed in Great Britain by Butler & Tanner Ltd., Frome and London

## Some of our Authors

W. H. DAVIES      AMBROSE BIERCE

LAWRENCE HOUSMAN

H. G. WELLS

SHERWOOD ANDERSON

JOHN MASEFIELD

GEORGE MOORE

WALTER PATER

A. E. COPPARD

PERCY LUBBOCK

LAFCADIO HEARN

EDMUND GOSSE

W. SOMERSET MAUGHAM

ARTHUR MASON

LIAM O'FLAHERTY

D. H. LAWRENCE

SAMUEL BUTLER

JOHN MIDDLETON MURRY

ANTON TCHEKOFF

NAOMI MITCHISON

MARK RUTHERFORD

STEPHEN GRAHAM

H. L. MENCKEN      E. H. YOUNG

J. W. N. SULLIVAN

HILAIRE BELLOC

JAMES JOYCE

WINWOOD READE

CHRISTOPHER MORLEY

IVAN TURGENEV

GUY DE MAUPASSANT

SINCLAIR LEWIS

JAMES HARVEY ROBINSON

THE TRAVELLERS' LIBRARY